Interlude
The Executive Office

Tal Bauer

A Tal Bauer Publication

www.talbauerwrites.com

ISBN: 9781549914348
Second Edition
10 9 8 7 6 5 4 3 2
Copyright © 2016 – 2017 Tal Bauer
Cover Art by Rocking Book Covers © Copyright 2017
Edited by Rita Roberts
First Published in 2016
Second Edition Published in 2017
Second Edition Published by Tal Bauer in the
United States of America

Dedication

To everyone who has enjoyed Jack and Ethan's story...
This one is for you.

Thank you, to all my readers. You are, quite simply, the best!

1

Des Moines, Iowa

"Twenty-seven credit cards, thirty thousand in hundreds—all with the exact same serial number—a credit card reader, and a laptop." United States Secret Service Special Agent Blake Becker whistled, shook his head, and glared at the two suspects in handcuffs sitting in the back of the Des Moines police cruiser. "We bagged another couple counterfeiters, huh?" He squinted at Ethan, snowflakes clinging to the ends of his eyelashes. Becker was twelve years younger than Ethan, and two years out of training at Rowley.

He was an infant.

Ethan said nothing. Becker's use of "we" was disingenuous. Ethan had put together the case after pulling files from three different states. He'd worked long, lonely hours in his cubicle, reading arrest records and statements until his eyeballs felt like they were bleeding. He'd tracked the washed bills, the counterfeit currency used in stores and banks across Iowa, Nebraska, and South Dakota. Built a timeline along one wall of his cube, tracking the rise of counterfeit bills in the tri-state area. Connected the dots, leading them to bust this run-down motel room and this raggedy team of counterfeiters.

And when he'd presented his case to Shepherd, the Special Agent in Charge of the small Des Moines Secret Service field office, Shepherd had assigned Blake Becker as the lead agent, putting him over Ethan. Days later, after Becker filed the affidavit in his own name, he and Ethan, along with the Des Moines police, broke down the door of the motel room and arrested two men in boxers and stained tank tops. One of the men had a mullet. The other, a greasy mustache and not much hair on the top of his head.

1

Two white news vans sloshed through the motel's parking lot. Muddy snowmelt splattered their sides, arching away from salt-crusted tires. On top of both, satellite dishes and transmission poles collected fat snowflakes beneath the leaden sky. Red-and-blue police lights swirled, giving a splash of color to the Midwestern gloom.

Becker jerked his head toward the new arrivals. "Media is here. Shepherd wants you to book it. Doesn't want you anywhere near the press."

Ethan kept his head down and headed for his Secret Service car, a nondescript Secret Service-issue sedan. He tucked his face into his scarf and his hands into the pockets of his trench coat.

If there was one thing Shepherd hated more than Ethan, it was the media attention he received. *"Secret Service Seduction turns to Presidential Regret?" "Ethan Reichenbach—Presidential Boyfriend or Dangerous Distraction?" "Boyfriend in Exile—Can Their Relationship Survive?" "Secret Service Hiding One of Their Own?"*

He slid into his car, slamming the door shut. He watched as the news crews set up around the motel parking lot and peered at the Special Agents and police processing the scene.

Ethan grabbed a pair of sunglasses and a ball cap from the passenger seat before he started his car. The sunglasses turned the drab gray sky almost black, but he kept them on as he backed up, maneuvering out of the crowd of police vehicles.

One of the reporters spotted his car leaving. She waved to her cameraman as she tore across the snowmelt, her brown boots sticky with slush. He tried to speed up, but she made it to his driver's side as he waited to turn onto the street.

"Mr. Reichenbach?" She knocked on the glass, and her cameraman scraped his lens over his window. "Mr. Reichenbach, can you talk about your involvement with the Des Moines Secret Service? What are your official duties?"

Ethan's jaw clenched. His fingers gripped the steering wheel. A few more seconds, a few passing cars, and he could peel out of there.

"How does it feel to be separated from the president? Are you and President Spiers still together? It's been a while since you were seen togeth—"

Finally, a break in the traffic. Ethan wanted to slam down on the accelerator, spin his wheels, and spray the reporter with mud and snow. But he couldn't. Everything—every single thing—he did was a reflection on Jack. A reflection on the president of the United States.

He revved his engine once, a warning, and then rolled forward. The camera squealed across his window. The reporter pounded on the glass, repeating her questions, almost shouting.

And then, he was out of the parking lot, back on the main road. He floored it, speeding off as the camera tracked him. A few blocks away, he ditched the sunglasses, throwing them onto the passenger seat.

Three months in exile. Three months of living in Des Moines, Iowa—away from Washington, DC, his friends, and the love of his life: Jack Spiers, president of the United States.

He thunked his head back against the headrest as his fingers kneaded the steering wheel. Three months of counting the days—and sometimes the hours—until he could see Jack again. He lived for the weekends, for Friday evening through Sunday night when he flew to DC, and the forty-eight hours that were just him and Jack. If he squinted while he was there, it was almost like it had been before everything came out, when they were hiding what they'd become together, and when Ethan had been Jack's Secret Service lead agent, at his side, always just a handbreadth away.

Day in and day out, they'd been at each other's side. Inseparable.

But every weekend ended, and Sunday night came, and with it, another flight back to Des Moines.

Ethan glared at the clock in his dash. It was too early to go back to his apartment and do anything but bang around within the empty walls and sulk, and too late to go back to work and expect to get anything done. Still, he turned for the office, heading back downtown. At the least, he could work out in the private gym for

3

agents assigned to the Federal Building. FBI, DEA, ATF, Secret Service, and Customs all shared one building.

All the agents also seemed to share in their wide-eyed, horrified distance from Ethan. He moved like a pariah, as though he'd been branded with a scarlet letter and anyone who came near him would suffer the same catastrophic fall from grace: from the most prestigious posting in the Secret Service—leading the presidential detail and personally protecting the president—to puzzling through small-time counterfeiting investigations out of a tiny field office in the Midwest.

And giving those investigations up to another agent, a junior agent, and running from the media.

He waited at the stoplight downtown just before the turn into the Federal Building's garage, listening to his wipers scrape snow off the windshield. The red traffic light blurred through the slush on his glass, tinting the inside of his sedan a dark crimson. Christmas lights stretched overhead, arching over streets and between buildings. Evergreen garlands clung to streetlights, and LED wreaths hung at every intersection. Over the weekend, Christmas had descended, just days after Thanksgiving.

If he'd known then what he knew now, would he do it all again? Make the same choices? Take the same risks? Kiss Jack—the president, his sworn duty, his job—and throw caution to the wind, going against his very bones, his dedication to his career, and the Secret Service?

The wipers slid against the glass again, squeaking, and the light turned green. His tires slipped on the snow, skidding out, but he slogged across the intersection and turned into the underground parking garage.

Of course he would. Those forty-eight hours each week with Jack made everything else worth it. Made bearable the isolation, the intrusive media, the sidelong glares and bitten-off conversations.

How his toes would curl as they kissed. Jack's smile, and the way his eyes lit up for Ethan alone. How Jack had looked at him when he'd burst into the Oval Office, gunfire cracking the air, taking out Jeff Gottschalk and Black Fox's operatives. Like Ethan was his whole world, the sun rising in the sky just for him.

Ethan had never loved anyone like he loved Jack. And he'd never been loved by anyone the way Jack loved him. It was still new, just six months old, but that love had remade Ethan's entire world. So far, he'd put up with anything. Everything. As long as Jack kept looking at him like that. Kept loving him like that.

But it had been over two weeks since he'd last been with Jack. "Every weekend" had turned into something else. Loneliness scratched at the base of his heart, and whispers of fear snaked down his bones.

Ethan wound through the underground garage and pulled into his assigned space, in the corner beneath the leaking air compressor, next to the dumpster that always smelled like stale piss.

Shepherd's car was still in his space. Great. Shepherd had probably already seen the footage of him running from the reporter, playing over and over on the local stations before being picked up by the national news for prime-time replay.

Shepherd would be pissed. More than pissed.

Sighing, Ethan badged into the building and onto the elevator, punching the button for the Secret Service's floor. When the elevator spat him out, he gave Agent Gibson a tight smile as he passed.

Gibson didn't smile back.

Ethan badged into the back door of the office, heading for his cube and his gym bag. On the way, he passed Shepherd's open office door.

The TV hanging on the wall in his office was on, images of Ethan driving out of the motel parking lot playing on repeat as the news anchor droned on about how evasive he'd been, how he hadn't answered any questions. About what his presence at the crime scene might mean. And, of course, wondering why he hadn't been seen with the president, or in DC, in weeks.

They were America's most scandalous couple, perhaps the world's. One question had been blaring from every radio, every gossip magazine, every late-night talk show host, almost from the moment they'd been photographed kissing on the North Lawn: were they still together?

Of course, the questioning had gotten louder these past few weeks.

Shepherd's glare fixed on Ethan. He pursed his lips as he perched on the edge of his desk, arms crossed over his slight pudge, a beer gut in the making. His tie was loose, the first few buttons at his neck undone.

Ethan grabbed his gym bag, slung it over his shoulder, and trudged to Shepherd's door. "Sir, I left as soon as they arrived. She chased me down. I wasn't trying to get in front of the cameras."

Shepherd pinched the bridge of his nose. "What did I do to deserve you?"

Ethan stayed silent.

"Thanks to this—" Shepherd gestured to the TV. "—the US Attorney is going to have to answer a million questions about you from whatever defense these guys cobble together. What you were doing there. Why you were involved."

"I put the case together—"

"And then it was given to Becker. *All* of it. The entire thing. Your fingerprints were stripped from it." Shepherd sighed again. "I don't want some criminal defense attorney trying to drag the president into one of our cases. Asking about what kind of special favors you get, or what the president is interested in, or how you don't play by the rules. We have to prove that everything you do is one hundred and ten percent aboveboard."

"Everything I've done here has been completely legal—"

"It's what you did *before* you got here." Shepherd fixed Ethan with another hard glare. "It's your character. The kinds of rules you break. A good defense attorney would rip you to shreds on the stand."

Ethan's chest felt like it had caved in. "I have never compromised an investigation for any reason."

"No." Shepherd snorted. "You just compromised the *president*."

Silence.

6

"Get out of here." Shepherd waved Ethan away, dismissing him as he stood. "I don't know what's going on with you and the president, and I don't want to know." His hand cut through the air, before Ethan spoke. He jerked his chin to the TV and the reporter musing about Ethan and Jack's relationship being on the rocks, or worse. "But you've gotten grumpier these past few weeks. And that's saying something." Shepherd squinted at him. "Go do something about that. If the media is going to hound you everywhere, you don't want them thinking you're a half breath away from snapping. Don't add fuel to the fire."

Clearing his throat, Ethan nodded once while Shepherd shuffled papers on his desk, dropping a stack of manila folders into his drawer. "Sir, I have a question."

Shepherd grunted.

"I submitted my vacation request for the holidays, but you haven't approved it yet. Is there a problem?" Ethan had lost vacation time in his demotion and had used up what was left flying back and forth to DC. He was scraping the last days he had to put together a trip back east over Christmas. It wasn't as long as he wanted, but it was what he had.

Shepherd barked out a harsh laugh, slamming a stack of papers down on his desk. "Why do you do this?"

"Sir?"

"Why do you pretend like you follow the rules? Like they even matter to you? You can break every rule we have, and nothing will happen to you."

"That's not who I am," Ethan growled. "I don't act that way."

"That's *exactly* who you are. And *exactly* how you acted."

"Sir, I don't get any special treatment—"

"Of course you do!" Shepherd cried. His hands rose as he shouted, his face turning red. "Why do you even bother coming in? Why do you put up the pretense of being an agent? You'd make it easier for everyone if you just *stopped* pretending!"

"I'm not pretending!" Ethan roared. "I'm doing my job!"

Shepherd laughed, long and loud. "You stopped doing your job the moment you compromised yourself and the president!"

"I am still an agent—"

"You're a Goddamn pain in my ass." Shepherd cut him off. "And I have *no clue* why you're still an agent. You shouldn't be. You should have been forced to turn in your badge and gun and been kicked out of the Service."

Ethan's jaw snapped shut, his teeth clicking together.

"Let me be perfectly clear. I don't give a shit what you do. Come to work. Don't come to work. Go on vacation for the entire month of December. Run away with the president and get drunk on some beach. I *don't* give a shit. Just stop wasting my time, okay?"

"Yes. Sir."

"Get out of my office."

His hand clenched around the strap of his duffel and his teeth ground together, but he strode out of Shepherd's office with his head held high. Rage thundered through him, deep in his veins.

There had better not be anyone in the gym downstairs. He had to get this out, pound it out into a punching bag until his knuckles split and he vomited in the corner. He had to get this out, because in three hours, Jack was going to call him on his computer, and he couldn't face Jack like this. Not about to fly apart, quaking with too much fury and raw shame. It hurt, God, it hurt.

But Jack couldn't see that. He couldn't ever see it.

2

White House
Washington DC

"Mr. President?"

Jack glanced up from his desk, reading glasses perched on the tip of his nose. Folders were spread out before him, analyses of the Caliphate's operations in Syria and Iraq, their attacks in Europe, and the strength of their forces in the Near East. Different projections of what the US military could do, both alone and with allies.

And, in one folder, an offer from President Sergey Puchkov. A potential alliance rooted in a UN resolution. The United States and Russia working together to fight the Caliphate. Could it be done?

Jack tossed his glasses on the desk and waved Pete Reyes, his press secretary, into the Oval Office. He stood, stretching his arms over his head and rolling his neck. His suit jacket was draped over the back of his office chair and his sleeves were rolled up.

"What's up, Pete?" Jack rested one hip against his desk as he crossed his arms with a tired smile.

Pete ambled to the center of the office. Dusk clung to DC beyond the Oval Office. Snowfall from an early storm blanketed the lawns, turning the world beyond into a winter wonderland. The snow seemed to encase the White House, an almost-shield from the real world. At least, Jack could pretend it was a shield.

"Just a few things before I head home, Mr. President." He flipped open his padfolio, lips pursed. "I've been sent to ask you one *last* time if you are *absolutely* sure you don't want to add some kind of LGBT or Pride element to the National Christmas Tree. Or to the White House. Or to any of the holiday décor we're about to throw on the walls."

Exhaling, Jack tipped his head back and closed his eyes. Pete waited.

Unease rumbled in Jack's gut. Coming out about him and Ethan had been the right thing to do. The honorable thing for Ethan's memory, when Jack thought he was gone, and for everything they had become together. He wasn't about to kick what they'd started, what they'd discovered, to the curb because it was politically expedient after Ethan's supposed death. He had started a real relationship with Ethan, and he'd meant it when he said he didn't care what the media, or the world, thought. He'd just wanted to fall in love with Ethan.

The agony of losing Ethan rubbed against the fatalistic pessimism he'd wallowed in after Ethiopia. It hadn't mattered that the country was in shock because of him. That Russia had distanced herself from their almost-alliance faster than the Iron Curtain had descended. That overnight, he'd gone from a promising potential to a late-night comedy sketch.

And then Ethan had come back.

And the world started to turn again.

It was different, trying to love Ethan in the spotlight instead of in their secreted, protected world from before. The media glare had intensified a thousandfold. Ethan had been stalked around DC, and reporters had hovered outside his condo before he transferred to Iowa. And then, when he did make the move, the media circus followed him. He lived in a small, secured apartment, set up specifically for government employees on long temporary duty, and the media lingered just beyond the gates. Camped outside the Federal Building in downtown Des Moines. Stalked him in the grocery stores. Tailed his car.

And everyone was trying to shove Jack into a place he didn't belong.

He wasn't stepping out of a closet. He wasn't admitting that he'd always desired men, had kept something hidden his whole life. That wasn't what he felt. And he wasn't trying to change the world. He just wanted to love Ethan, and no one seemed to accept that.

Everyone wanted something from him, some kind of statement or stance or public commitment. Something that tried to politicize his personal life, and his love.

Hell, Jack didn't even know what to call himself. The world had decided on "Gay President of the United States", which wasn't right, but Jack couldn't get his brain started to figure out what *was* correct. He'd fallen for Ethan, so was he now open to falling for any man? That thought derailed quickly. He couldn't think about any *person* other than Ethan, man or woman. He didn't want to imagine the possibility that they wouldn't work out.

But maybe this was something new about himself. Something he hadn't known he was, all these years. So, he had tried to surreptitiously scope out some of the more attractive men working at the White House. The Marine Corps guards and the attachés in the Situation Room. One or two of the political directors. He'd let his eyes linger on their shoulders, their waists, their asses.

Nothing.

But when he thought about Ethan's shoulders, the flex of his muscles when he was working out, or the long lines of his tight thighs, his strong, rounded ass and trim waist—

Well, he'd learned he couldn't let his mind wander in Cabinet meetings any longer. There were only so many times he could ask someone to stay after for a sidebar conversation while he desperately tried to will his erection back down.

Was it *just* Ethan? Just their lives crashing into one another and the forced isolation of the White House mixed with the intensity of presidential protection creating a perfect cauldron for their feelings to develop?

Though, his sexual attraction to Ethan hadn't developed until after Ethan had kissed him and the possibility had been planted in his brain. Was he sexually attracted to Ethan because he'd already fallen for him, in a way? Was their close friendship a bridge to his heart and his love?

How did he simplify who he was and how he felt to one word, one phrase? Was it even possible?

What was true was this: he'd taken a risk, the biggest risk he'd ever taken in his life, and everything that came after had made him, on the one hand, the happiest he'd ever been, and on the other, the most frustrated and irate he'd ever been, too.

He was madly in love with Ethan. That, at the end of the day, was true.

"Can't we focus on something else?" Jack sighed, one hand scrubbing over his face. "Anything else? The country has been through a major shock. We're getting ready to go to war. I'm off to the UN to try to build an alliance for the first time in twenty years. There are people we need to honor. Victims of these terrorists, of Madigan, and a world that did nothing for too long." Jack shook his head. "Those are the real issues. It's not all about me. It can't be. I'm not that interesting."

Pete chewed on his lip, his eyebrows slowly rising as Jack spoke.

Jack exhaled. "All right. Hit me."

"You and Mr. Reichenbach are also a real issue. You're the first out—"

Jack groaned.

"First out president, and you started a relationship while in the White House. It's news. Everyone wants to know more."

"Great. My first big achievement. Uniting the people in their fascination with my sex life."

"You're a lot of things to a lot of people. Crazy, deranged—" Pete grinned as Jack chuckled. "And inspirational," he finished.

"Oh, don't make me feel worse. Please."

"You want your private life private. I *get* it. I'm just not sure that it's realistic." Pete's gaze softened.

"It has to be," Jack breathed. "Ethan's suffering too much as it is. He's not a part of this media circus like you and I are. His whole job was to stay *out* of the spotlight."

"Speaking of him. Des Moines news media picked him up at an arrest today. The Secret Service was catching some counterfeiters. They spotted Mr. Reichenbach and chased his car down. National media is playing the clip over and over."

Jack cupped his hands over his face. "He doesn't deserve this. God… I just want to be with him, our way, in private, and dedicate everything else I have and am to this office. Can't that be enough?"

Pete smiled tightly. "We can try, Mr. President."

"You once told me that I should minimize this. Toss it aside, act like it was meaningless. 'Do a Clinton,' you said. Now you think I'm inspirational?"

"I… didn't know how much it meant to you. You and him, I mean." Pete cleared his throat. "You weren't saying much at the time and no one really knew anything. Jeff, uhh, seemed to know a bit." Pete coughed and talked fast, getting past Jeff Gottschalk's name in a hurry as Jack glared. "But I didn't know what Reichenbach meant to you until you told the world you guys were in love." Pete shrugged. "But you did. You changed the world in forty-five seconds. And now we have to work with that."

"Do you want to?"

Pete stared at Jack. "Do I want to…"

"This isn't what you signed up for," Jack said softly. "You joined my team when I was in the Senate because you knew I was going to make a run for the White House. You wanted to be the White House press secretary, and you worked your ass off, Pete. You did." Jack smiled but looked down, one foot scuffing against the floor. "I think I broke a lot of people's dreams when I said what I said. I put all of us in a whole new world. None of you asked for this. We're on our heels now. Eight years has gone down to the next three." He looked up, an apology in his eyes. "You wanted to announce peace in the Middle East, a renewed America, and a stronger world. Now you're dodging questions about my sex life."

"At *least*, no joke, thirty times a day. You should really see some of these questions." Pete whistled, and his tone was serious, but he broke into a smile, chuckling. He calmed a moment later, closing his padfolio and holding it over his chest. "Mr. President, I wanted to be part of a team that was going to change the world. I knew you were that man. That you would be the president to do the next great thing."

He shrugged again. "So it's not the way I imagined. But I *am* a part of something amazing. Something I am damn proud to represent."

Slowly, Jack smiled. "Thanks. Thank you. I'm… *really* glad you're here."

Pete held out his hand. Jack took it, gripping tight. A moment later, he and Pete pulled back at the same time, snapping and pointing at each other in unison. It had started as a joke, but they kept doing it along the campaign trail, all the way up to the day they moved into the White House. Now, almost a year later, their ritual made a comeback. Jack laughed.

"You should get going, Mr. President. It's almost nine."

Jack pushed off the desk and pulled out his phone to check the time. "That it is!" Grinning, he flipped his folders closed and grabbed his suit jacket. "I've got to get ready for my date."

3

Des Moines

Ethan plopped down in front of his computer and logged in to Skype ten minutes early. He had a beer next to the keyboard and a bag of ice resting on the knuckles of his right hand, hidden out of sight in his lap. In the gym, he'd pummeled the punching bag until his knuckles had split and stained his wraps, and one of the other agents had pulled him back from going even harder.

He'd showered at his apartment, made a sandwich, and sat at his desk to wait for Jack's call.

Butterflies tangled in his stomach, each and every time. Three months they'd been doing the same routine, and still, Ethan wondered when it would all start to fade. When Jack wouldn't make the call. Or when he would realize that he really didn't want to put up with all the crap that loving Ethan brought.

At five minutes to eight, his computer chimed. Jack calling, and he was early.

His throat clenched as he ran his fingers through his damp hair and straightened in his seat. He'd obsessed over the angle of the monitor for the first call, stacking it up on books until he thought it looked right, and he didn't look too tired, or the angle didn't highlight the gray poking through at his temples. God, he wasn't used to being the young one.

He never knew what to wear. Jack had seen him in a suit every day at the White House. Should he be casual? He didn't want Jack to think he didn't care enough to not look good for him. Shirtless? Was that too forward? Maybe not for another guy, but Jack wasn't just anyone. He settled on a shirt that was a bit too tight, wriggling into it, and his boxers. Jack wouldn't see below the waist. They didn't do that. Jack was classy. And Ethan didn't push his luck.

Clearing his throat, he clicked to answer, smiling nervously.

Jack's brilliant grin filled his screen. He was sitting on his bed in the Residence, one leg tucked up to his chest, dressed down in his suit pants and his white T-shirt. He was tired; Ethan could tell. He had his reading glasses on and the very beginnings of dark circles beneath his eyes.

Jack was gorgeous. He made Ethan's heart skip faster, made his body burn. "Hey," he breathed. And just like that, he was finally smiling, for real.

"Hey you." Jack tugged his laptop closer; the screen wobbled and then resettled, Jack's face closer to the camera. His eyes dropped to the center of the screen, seeming to linger over Ethan's chest and shoulders. "How was your day?" he asked, dragging his gaze back up to Ethan's face.

"Good." Ethan shrugged. His knuckles stung beneath the ice baggie.

"Did you get your warrant? Catch the bad guys you've been chasing?"

Ethan chuckled. He looked down, rolling a pen over his desk. "Yeah, the team got the warrant this morning. Busted in on the counterfeiters in the motel room they were living out of." He left out how he'd had to turn over the whole investigation to a man twelve years his junior, a newbie to the Secret Service. Frowning, he cleared his throat. "The, ah, media found me at the scene. I didn't get out in time." He snorted. "Des Moines Secret Service financial crimes investigations have never made the national news, until now." Silence. He looked up.

Jack was gazing at him, an apology in his eyes. "I saw the clip. I'm sorry, Ethan."

"You don't have anything to be sorry for."

"You don't deserve to be hounded like that. I wish everyone would ignore us."

Ethan looked away.

"If we keep ignoring them, maybe they'll give up?" Jack smiled hopefully.

"We can try."

"Let's be boring." Jack winked. "Let's be really, really boring."

"You couldn't be boring if you tried." Ethan laughed. "It's not in you."

"I can do anything I set my mind to. I'm sure I could figure out how to be boring. I'll just ask Senator Bryant." He winked again. "Or Congressman Wills."

Laughing again, Ethan felt some of the day's tension uncoil from between his shoulders. "What about you? How was your day?"

Sighing, Jack scrubbed his hands over his face and through his hair. Dirty-blond and brunet strands stuck up at crazy angles. "Oh, just trying to figure out how to put together the right proposal for the invasion force when I go to the UN next week. General Bradford and the Joint Chiefs were war-gaming today, presenting me with... God, too many options. They have a model for every possible country joining us. Did you know that?"

"We all like to be thorough when we're presenting you with options." It was Ethan's turn to wink.

"It's too much." Jack pitched sideways on the bed, dragging his laptop with him. He propped himself up on his elbow, staring at the camera and Ethan. "I'm going to talk to President Puchkov about his offer. A combined Russian-American invasion force? A joint operation? And he wants us to take it to the UN together? I almost can't believe it. He brought me a glass of champagne and a red folder with this proposal tucked in at the G20's closing reception. Said it was for me to read later and walked away. *Classic* Russian style."

"Could it be a trap?" Ethan frowned. President Puchkov hadn't been the most amazing world leader to Jack in his first year. Taunts before the NATO Summit in Prague and then a tentative alliance ripped away after Jack's revelation about their relationship.

"I don't think so. I think it's his attempt to rebuild what we were doing before. We haven't really spoken much at all since—" Jack shrugged.

Ethan squirmed. Jack never put words to describe what the press conference outing him and Jack was.

"But a joint deployment to combat the Caliphate, and under the auspices of the UN? That's about as public an alliance and a commitment as you can get these days in global politics." Jack shrugged one shoulder. "Maybe it's his way of reaching out."

Jack had been at the G20 Summit the week before—the week of Thanksgiving—mixing and mingling with his fellow world leaders. It was his first international trip since their relationship became public knowledge, and everyone had wondered what the world's reactions would be. Newspapers speculated on who would shake his hand and who would not. Scott, Ethan's best friend and head of Jack's Secret Service detail after Ethan's transfer-in-exile, had endlessly bitched about the security nightmare over the phone to Ethan.

And Ethan had chewed his nails to nubs, watching Jack on TNN on his phone at his Des Moines office and obsessing over the headlines from the Summit. His fellow agents saw him watching the livestream in the breakroom, huddled over a cup of coffee and his cell with headphones jammed deep in his ears. They steered away from him, saying nothing.

He and Jack had lost the weekend before and the weekend after the G20, and all of Thanksgiving. Thanksgiving was an American holiday, and the G20 did not care about such things when planning their meeting. But, Jack had ordered a family-style Thanksgiving dinner for his entire staff while on the trip, and he'd Skyped Ethan from their long table as everyone ate. Scott and Daniels had made faces at him in between bites. Even Welby had cracked a tiny grin. It had been so Jack, so effortlessly warm and thoughtful.

Ethan had eaten leftover cold pizza and watched football in between waiting for texts.

Jack came back to the US on a Saturday and went straight to Texas, spending one night with his parents in the Austin suburbs. Sunday, three days ago, he flew back to DC.

Loneliness pitted Ethan's heart. They hadn't been apart this much ever, not since Ethan's fight back from the grave after Ethiopia. He *missed* Jack, and he missed his friends. His old life. Everything he'd known, for over a decade, had been wrapped up in DC and in the White House.

He tried to push away the creeping sense of isolation as he and Jack kept chatting back and forth, moving from politics to White House gossip.

"Oh!" Jack waggled his eyebrows. "Jeannette, that blonde reporter from the *Herald*? She got engaged to Benjamin in the Domestic Policy section today. He did it in the briefing room."

"Really?" Ethan grinned. "Poor Vinny."

"Vinny?"

"Secret Service. Vinny Brewsky. Good guy from Brooklyn. He was dating her for a while. Man, he was gone for her. She dumped him, though. She had her gaze set higher than just the Secret Service."

Jack pressed his hand to his chest, his eyes wide. He *tsked* three times as Ethan chuckled.

"Lawrence tells me they're going to start decorating tomorrow. He looks a little... nervous." Jack frowned.

"You have no idea." Ethan couldn't hold back his smile. "An army will descend on the White House tomorrow. Volunteers, most of whom are about as dedicated to their mission as any Spec Ops soldier could ever be. It will be an invasion of Santa hats. It's unbelievable."

Jack laughed. "I remember coming to the White House when I was in the Senate and being awed. I didn't think about how all of it went up."

"You've seen ants build something, right? It's like that." Ethan's fingers waggled in front of the screen. "Just accept, right now, that glitter is going to be a part of your life for the next six weeks. It will be in the air you breathe and the food you eat."

"Maybe I'll call in sick tomorrow."

"It's—" Something grabbed Ethan's heart and squeezed. He looked down, picking at his bag of ice. "It's gorgeous, actually," he said softly. "It's amazing, what they do. When everything is up, the whole place is transformed." Memories flashed as he swallowed, his throat tight. "It's probably my favorite time of the year there. I mean, it's a beating, because there are so many visitors, and so many parties. We work all the time, but—" Ethan pressed his lips together. "But it's great. It's the best time of the year at the White House."

He glanced up, finding Jack's soft gaze on the monitor. "Sounds amazing. I can't wait to experience it with you."

Ethan smiled. He looked away.

"I can't wait until Friday, either. It's been too long." Jack sighed again, dramatically. "Next year, I'll just have to bring you with me if they schedule the G20 over Thanksgiving."

Next year. Next Thanksgiving. Ethan's smile grew until his cheeks ached, burned, no doubt flushed crimson with his combined joy and embarrassment.

"You've got the tree lighting this Friday night, right?" The National Christmas Tree, on the Ellipse near the White House, was decorated every year for Christmas, along with smaller trees for every state and territory. The president—and historically the first family—always lit the tree the first weekend in December. It was a fun, festive event, and past presidents had really gotten into the evening. Jack would be just as enthralled, feeding off the energy of the crowd.

"Yeah." Jack nodded. "I'll be there when your plane lands. Scott said he's sending another agent to pick you up, since he needs almost everyone for the tree lighting. But you're not going to be forgotten. He'll bring you back here, and I'll escape as soon as I can."

"You should enjoy yourself. Have fun. It's a great event."

"I want to enjoy myself with *you*." Jack's eyes glittered. "I don't want to miss a single moment that you're here. And, do you really think I'll be able to even string a sentence together once I know you're home?"

Ethan chuckled. There was no talk about him joining Jack at the tree lighting. They'd decided long ago that they would keep their relationship far, far away from the public eye. No comments. No media. No public appearances. Maybe it was hiding. But it was their plan.

"Day after tomorrow." Jack kept grinning, kept staring at Ethan as though he was something special. "I need a time machine. Need to speed up time. Thursday is just a waste. Let's skip it. Go straight to Friday."

Laughing, Ethan agreed and then watched Jack try to smother a yawn. "It's late," he said softly. "You should go to bed."

"I am in bed."

"You should get some sleep." A smile played over Ethan's lips. "Presidents need their beauty rest."

Jack ran a hand through his hair, striking a pose as he lay on his side. "I'm gorgeous."

"Yes. You are."

That made Jack pause. He bit his lip, a flush rising on his cheekbones, and his gaze turned heated. "Friday." One hand reached for the screen, a finger tracing over Ethan's face on his laptop as he blew a kiss. "I love you, Ethan."

Ethan had to fight through his clenched throat to speak. "Love you too."

"Sleep well. Talk to you tomorrow." His hand slowly drew back, hovering over the mousepad. Any moment, he'd end the call. Ethan stared at him, breathing fast through his mouth, trying to make the seconds stretch longer. Trying to keep the image of Jack in his eyes forever, as if they could stop time and never have to hang up.

And then the screen went dark.

The ice in his bag had completely melted and his hand and boxers were soaked. His untouched beer was warm. Ethan trudged to his tiny kitchen and dumped both in the sink. As he dried his hand, he stared at the three pictures of him and Jack he had on his fridge.

Day after tomorrow. And then he'd see Jack again.

In the morning, Agent Becker texted Ethan, telling him to meet at the jail for interrogations of the suspects. He headed across town sipping his coffee in the predawn darkness. He'd finally left early enough to dodge the reporters who liked to huddle outside his apartment complex and snap pictures of his morning commute.

Jack texted on the way, sending over a selfie from the Oval Office. Him at his desk, grinning like the Cheshire cat.

36 hours till I kiss you again!!!!

Ethan couldn't smother his smile, and he didn't try.

At the jail, Becker met him with an arched eyebrow and a bemused expression. Ethan tried to ratchet back his radiating happiness. He was usually dour and closed off at the office, but Jack's texts could make his whole world spin faster. And one like that, well.

"Des Moines PD picked up an accomplice of our perps last night. Female, nineteen years old. She was casing the crime scene in a Hyundai. PD followed her and pulled her over. She had twenty grand in counterfeit hundreds in her trunk and five pounds of marijuana. Serial numbers on the bills match the ones from the perps." He passed over a folder. Inside were photocopies of the forged bills, front and back.

They badged inside, waving to the sheriffs in the bullpen as another escorted them to the interview rooms. The counterfeit bills were extremely high quality. Other than the repeating serial number, a UV detector would be the only way to catch that the hundreds weren't actually hundreds. They'd stripped out the ink from five- and one-dollar bills, keeping the paper with the embedded security strips and foil holograms, before reprinting the bills to look like hundreds. It was a sophisticated setup, something seen more in organized crime rings, and not in a dumpy motel in the upper Midwest.

They stopped at the end of the hall. Two doors stood across from each other. "I'll start with the girl." Becker nodded to the other door. "The first guy is all set up in there for you to warm up. Remember, you're not really here. No cameras, no records."

He headed in, giving the sheriff at the door a tight smile before he settled down at the table bolted to the floor in the center of the interrogation room. The prisoner was already seated on the other side, the chain between his handcuffs locked to the steel table. Ethan dropped the prisoner's file on the table and peeled out of his thick overcoat and scarf.

"Holy shit," the prisoner breathed, as if he'd just won a prizefight. "God-fucking *damn it*. It's *you*! You're the president's faggot!"

Ethan bit down on the inside of his lip as he draped his coat over the back of the metal folding chair. At the door, the sheriff's eyes narrowed.

"God*damn!*" Cackling, the prisoner rocked in his chair, curled over with one fist over his mouth. "You're a Goddamn faggot celebrity, you know that? Fucking everywhere. Every Goddamn magazine I see has your picture on it. Every-fucking-body around here talks about you." He leaned forward, his fingers tapping against the table. "And now you're here with me? My lucky fucking day."

Ethan sat slowly, straightening his tie. Flipped open the folder. So much for being under the radar. "Aaron Curtis, from Sioux Falls, South Dakota. You made a name for yourself up there. Racked up quite a record. Managed to piss off just about everyone you met."

Aaron grinned. Cracked teeth flashed, yellowed from meth.

"Worked your way out to Pine Ridge, bootlegging moonshine and running meth through the reservation until the Tribal Police drove you out. Did time in three different jails. You have quite the rap sheet, Mr. Curtis."

"I must be some hot shit to get you in here to talk to me." Aaron kept grinning like a crazed clown.

"How did you figure out how to counterfeit these bills? Where'd you get the materials to produce this kind of quality counterfeit? Those aren't easy to come by."

"Does the president know you're talking to me? He know all about me?" Ethan stared as Aaron laughed himself silly.

"Your record is long but unimpressive. You're a bully. A thug. Guys like you don't become master counterfeiters—"

"*Master* counterfeiter. I like it."

23

Ethan kept going, ignoring the interruption. "They don't build labs in their motel rooms from thin air. Everything you got, you got from someone. You're just the small fish at the end of the line."

Aaron's eyes flashed. He tried to pound his chest, but the handcuff chain jerked. "I'm a big fucking deal, asshole."

"You're really not."

"You're here, aren't you?" Aaron spread his hands and sniffed.

"I don't need to be." Ethan stood, grabbing his coat.

"Wait. All right, wait."

Ethan sat. He leaned back, crossed his legs, and ran his tongue over his teeth. "Where did you get your materials from?"

Aaron looked sideways, toward the sheriff. He grinned down at the table and then steeled his expression before he looked up. "I got a question first," he said, his eyes earnest, his voice serious. He leaned in.

Ethan frowned.

Aaron's fingers tapped the cold steel. "Did you turn the president gay, or did he already like sucking cock before you fucked him in the ass?"

Lightning fast, Ethan reached for Aaron, grabbing him and tangling his fingers in his mullet before slamming him face-first into the steel table. Bones crunched, and as Ethan jumped to his feet, Aaron wheeled back, blood pouring from his nose.

"Motherfucker!" Aaron bellowed. "I'll fucking kill you!" He tried to leap up, but the sheriff was suddenly there, and his fist slammed into Aaron's stomach, doubling him over. "Jesus, you're clumsy," the sheriff grunted. He nodded Ethan toward the door.

"Clumsy motherfucker," the sheriff said. "Falling all over the place."

"I didn't fucking fall!" Aaron stood, the sound of a wad of spit forming in the back of his throat.

The sheriff grabbed the back of his neck and shoved him down on the table. Aaron's cheek smashed against the cold steel. "You fell again, you clumsy asshole. And was that a threat I heard?

Threatening a federal agent is five years in a federal pen added on to your sentence. Want to see how many more years we can add?"

"That fucker—"

"You tripped. And you didn't make a threat."

Ethan shut the door as Aaron spewed. His heart was racing, galloping out of his chest, and his hands shook. That was stupid. That was epically fucking stupid. God, he couldn't let assholes get under his skin like that. All someone had to do was insult Jack a little bit and Ethan would lose control. If he kept that up, he'd be tanking Jack's presidency even further in no time at all.

He shouldered his way into the observation room beside Becker's interrogation. The two-way mirror revealed a flustered Becker flipping through a thin folder and a bored, sour-faced woman. Her file had said she was nineteen and her name was Doreen Watts. She was a teenager, but years on the street and the results of a long line of track marks on her arms had aged her.

He watched for a few minutes and then headed into Becker's interrogation. Not like he was any kind of expert on questioning, especially after his amazing performance with Aaron, but he had more mileage than Becker. As long as he kept his cool.

Becker glared as he entered.

"Oh my God." Doreen sat forward, her mouth falling open. She'd been chewing at her nails, bored, but perked up. "You're him."

Jesus. Ethan exhaled. Stared at her. Blinked.

Doreen grinned. "You're the president's boyfriend." She bit her lip. "I read every article about you two."

Becker rolled his eyes.

"It's the modern love story!" Doreen snapped at Becker. "Fucking Cinderella!"

Ethan arched his eyebrows. Doreen spun toward him, her chin propped in her palm as she gazed at him. She had crazy eyes.

"You working with these clowns?"

She squinted, but said nothing. *That's a yes.*

25

"What's the source for your materials? Aaron isn't a master counterfeiter. He's nothing. How'd you guys figure out how to turn these bills out so well?"

Her gaze darkened as her smile faded. Her teeth dragged over her lip and she looked down, then away.

Interesting. She was the link. She had the information.

"You work with us, we'll work with you." Ethan gestured to himself and Becker, then to her. Becker had shut up and was watching him with something other than disdain, for once.

Doreen looked up, smiling again. It didn't reach her eyes, though. "Listen, sugar butt. I love your Cinderella story. But I'm never gonna snitch on Mother."

4

Ethan almost vibrated out of his skin as he parked his sedan at Des Moines's airport. A light snow was falling from the gray sky, just enough to coat the sidewalks but not delay any flights. He wrapped his scarf tighter around his neck, shoved his hands into his black wool overcoat, and headed for the gate.

A gaggle of reporters camped at the entrance, snapping pictures of him striding toward the security checkpoint. Shouted questions bombarded him all around, and angry-looking National Guardsmen kept the reporters back. Ethan flashed his badge and made his way through security as fast as possible, escaping down the terminal and leaving behind the madness of the media.

Jack had texted him that morning, a selfie he'd taken in bed right as he woke up. *Tomorrow, I wake up with you next to me.* <3

He never knew how to respond to Jack's effortlessly loving texts. He was more used to men sending him dick pics and stats, not countdowns until they saw each other again and joyous smiles. But he loved it, every single bit, and he'd sent back a pic of his packed duffel with a thumbs-up. He'd been packed for days.

His natural gruffness kept people away from him as he sat outside a coffee shop at a bistro table across from his gate while he waited. A man he recognized from every one of his flights showed up at the gate within three minutes, his eyes flicking to Ethan once and then away. He stayed at Ethan's right, ninety degrees off, inside twenty yards. Smiling, Ethan stared down at his coffee cup. Same guy, every flight, back and forth from Des Moines to DC.

He knew a fellow federal agent when he saw one. Seemed he had a shadow.

Forty-five minutes later, they were boarding. Ethan got on first, since he was flying armed, and the mystery man followed not long after. The rest of the flight filed in, ignoring Ethan for the most part. He was up in first class, next to the window. Jack had paid to upgrade all his tickets from coach to first class, unbeknownst to Ethan at the time. He certainly couldn't afford weekly first-class flights. But Jack had paid for the upgrades, and it was almost like they were splitting the cost.

He sent Jack a selfie of him on the plane. *[soon!]*

As they were taxiing to the runway, his cell buzzed. A reply from Jack: a long line of Xs and Os and a dozen smiley faces.

Washington DC

Twenty thousand people had been granted tickets through the National Tree's Holiday Lottery, and they swelled into President's Park on the Ellipse, just south of the White House. The National Tree lived on the Ellipse, and for the past month, had been spruced and trimmed by the Park Service and decked out to the nines. It was ready for its big moment.

Each year, the president was supposed to pick a theme for the National Tree, and for the surrounding fifty-six smaller trees. Themes were usually decided in February, and an army of engineers worked all year long to bring that theme to life. Jack had initially decided to go with a "'Twas the Night Before Christmas" theme.

But then, Madigan had struck. The nation, and the world, had reeled. Shock had gripped everyone, the very real threat of a nuclear attack striking their homeland oh-so-narrowly averted.

Too many had been lost to terror and to war, for decades. Too many deaths and shattered lives. Jack had experienced all of that horror, all of that fear, the devastation when someone he loved had been ripped away by terror and evil in the world, and he wasn't going to let a single other person feel the way he'd felt. Not if he could do something about it.

He'd started three months ago, building support for an international coalition to strike against the Caliphate in the Near East. Russia's return and President Puchkov's offer had surprised him, but Puchkov's proposal to combine their military forces in the operation was solid. He was making an honest offer for an alliance, a partnership between their nations that could change the world.

He and Puchkov would be at the UN next week, presenting to the world their proposed resolution for combat operations. If everything went right, by the end of the year, he and President Puchkov would be leading the fight to clear the world of darkness and terror.

It was another in the long line of actions and causes he'd thrown himself into over the years, a way to honor and memorialize his wife's death and her sacrifice in the war. Something he could do to help the world.

Action was one way to honor the fallen. Memorials and memories were another. After Madigan, Jack had ordered a change in theme for the National Tree. Gone was the cute children's story.

Instead, the tree had been outfitted with a white LED for every life that had been lost to terror attacks around the world for that year. On the smaller surrounding trees, red, white, and blue lights twinkled for every member of the armed forces lost over the past two decades, broken out by state and territory. And, stretching under the snow on the South Lawn, long lines of ghostly lights twinkled for the civilian lives lost in the tumult of the wars and occupations.

It was an odd evening, a celebration that had historically been festive and full of fun made heavier, more solemn, at times. Jack listened to the singers perform a mix of Christmas songs and memorials that had people dancing one moment and wiping away tears the next. The stage was outfitted with red, white and blue, and gold and green, and snow still blanketed the park and the White House. His breath fogged in front of his face, but the night was clear and crisp. The crowd blazed with life and energy.

When he strode across the stage to deliver his short speech, the crowd leaped to their feet, cheering raucously for five minutes straight. He tried to wave them down, but they kept going, and he ended up just standing there, letting their applause roll over him as his throat clenched and he blinked fast, trying to hold himself together.

"Good evening, Washington, DC!" he cried into the microphone, once he could be heard. "And good evening, America!" More cheers and applause. He waved to the crowd, smiling.

Near the end of his speech, his phone buzzed in his pocket, over and over again. The alarm he'd set for Ethan's plane touching down. Swallowing, he plowed ahead with his closing remarks and then wrapped it all up. "Happy holidays, America. Let the season begin!" There was a comical button on the podium, and he pressed it with as much fanfare as he could. Someone watched him from a control booth nearby, and they flicked the massive switch controlling the lights on the National Tree, the state trees, and the lights on the south lawn. Everything lit up at once, a burst of glowing light refracting off the snow and the starlit sky. Cheers and applause rose, and the Marine Corps band dove into a swing rendition of "Jingle Bells."

Waving, Jack escaped the center stage, heading down Scott's prescribed path and back to the protective clutches of the Secret Service at the base of the stage. Agents Daniels and Caldwell were waiting for him, as was the media. He had to say a few words, say something to the perky blonde reporter waiting for him. It was part of the evening.

His phone buzzed in his pocket again. A text message. *Ethan.*

Ethan was there, in DC, possibly already at the White House. It was time to go. He needed to be with Ethan.

Jack pasted a smile on his face and hovered next to the blonde reporter. "Hi!" he said, beaming into the camera.

"Mr. President, what a wonderful evening. How are you doing tonight?"

"Great! This is a fantastic tradition, and it's a real honor to be here and be a part of it all." He clapped his lips shut as his cell phone buzzed again.

"As we approach the holiday season, Mr. President, everyone is watching and waiting for the UN's vote on your proposal to combat the Caliphate—how they've seized so much of the Middle East, and their terror attacks around the world. Can you comment on the situation?"

"Terrorism is a global concern, and building a united global response to that has been one of my biggest goals. I have some more information on the scope of our alliance that I will be speaking about in the coming days." He smiled into the camera and nodded, his silent cue that the interview was through.

"Mr. President, we noticed that Ethan Reichenbach was not in attendance tonight, and he hasn't been seen with you in several weeks. You didn't spend the Thanksgiving holiday together. What's the status of your relationship with Mr. Reichenbach?"

His smile tightened. "I don't comment on my personal life." He nodded again and tried to reach quietly for Daniels, just behind him.

"Would you say whether you two are or are not still in a relationship?"

Daniels pulled him back, as if whispering in his ear. Jack nodded seriously and then turned to the reporter. "Have to run. Happy holidays, everyone!" He waved for the camera before turning and following Daniels's lead through the crowd, Caldwell and Welby on his heels. A line of black SUVs with flashing red-and-blue lights squealed to a stop on the Ellipse in front of him. Daniels guided Jack to one in the middle, jogging through the crunching snow with his hand on the small of Jack's back.

Scott was in the front seat, next to Agent Beech. Jack smiled at both agents as he climbed into the back. Daniels shut the door and rapped twice on the roof, and then Scott pulled away.

He pulled out his cell, thumbing open the text messages from Ethan. *[I'm here.]*

[You look good on TV :)]

His heart skipped a beat as the White House loomed closer, and they headed for the security gate. Ethan was inside. He was finally there. Finally back where he belonged, in DC, at the White House, and—soon—by Jack's side.

I'm on my way!

Ethan bit his lip and slid his phone into his pocket. He was dressed down in jeans and his black sweater—the one that hugged all his muscles—and pacing at the top of the Grand Staircase. Any minute, Jack would be back. He exhaled, rubbed his palms down his jeans, and pivoted, pacing again.

Hanier had picked him up at the airport, shaking his hand before pulling him in for a quick hug. They'd piled into the SUV, and Hanier had turned on the red and blues, making fast time back to the White House while they caught up, until his friend and fellow agent dropped him at the private entrance with a wink.

Footsteps echoed over the marble floor of the Cross Hall below. He spun, blowing air out of his hollowed cheeks as he waited. The stairs were U-shaped, with a landing halfway down at the bend.

Ethan spotted Jack rushing up the lower half, taking the stairs two at a time, his black overcoat flapping behind him.

Jack rounded the curve, one hand on the bannister, and looked up. His eyes met Ethan's.

He stilled.

And then broke into a thousand-watt smile, his whole face lit from within. He pounded up the last of the stairs, his gaze fixed to Ethan's until he came to a stop right in front of him, so close their chests brushed.

"Hey," Jack breathed. His eyes glittered as he gave Ethan a long once-over. He leaned forward, as if he was going to fall into Ethan, but caught himself, rocking back on the balls of his feet.

"Hey." Ethan's grin was shy. He couldn't look away, but he couldn't move either. For weeks, all he'd wanted was to reach for Jack, hold him in his arms, and now that he was inches away, he was struck immobile, frozen by everything Jack was. His fingers tingled and his palms twitched as his eyes roamed over Jack and his stunning smile.

Jack glanced up and grinned.

A sprig of mistletoe had been tacked to the archway above.

"I put it up this morning," Jack confessed. "Dragged a chair from the dining room."

"The Jefferson chairs?" Ethan frowned. "Jack! You're the president. You shouldn't be standing on a chair at the top of the staircase. What if you fell?"

Jack laughed, throwing his head back, and reached for Ethan. He gripped Ethan's biceps, tugging him close, and then stroked up Ethan's shoulders and behind his neck. "I've missed you *so* much," he breathed, right before he captured Ethan's lips in a heated kiss.

Ethan's frozen fear shattered. His arms wrapped around Jack, pulling him flush to his body as their kiss continued, turned searing. Jack sucked at Ethan's lower lip. Ethan grabbed Jack's overcoat and tugged it off his shoulders.

Jack shoved him backward, starting him down the hall, and reached for the hem of his sweater.

Ethan dropped Jack's overcoat and then his suit jacket in a line as they moved, never breaking their kiss. Jack's tie came off next, then Ethan's sweater, and Jack's hands roamed over Ethan's chest. Jack's lips traveled down Ethan's neck, sucking on his collarbone, his chest, as Ethan fumbled with Jack's belt. They were stumbling down the hall, a trail of clothes in their wake, but it wasn't fast enough. Ethan burned, wanting more.

His back hit the wall, hard, as Jack shoved him, burying his face in Ethan's chest and leaving a trail of hot, wet kisses from his nipple to his ear and then back to his lips. Jack's hands worked at Ethan's jeans as Ethan shivered and pushed Jack's pants down. The black fabric fell to the floor, pooling around his feet.

Jack toed out of his shoes and laced their fingers, pressing Ethan's hands to the wall over his head. He sucked Ethan's lower lip into his mouth again, grinning, and then slowly slid down Ethan's body while he tugged Ethan's jeans off. Fuck, his body felt so good, hot and solid against Ethan, pressed tight with every inch of his slither.

Ethan's head hit the wall as Jack's lips closed over his hard cock through the thin fabric of his boxers.

"Jack…"

Jack winked up at him, lips wrapped around his cockhead.

33

Ethan pulled Jack to his feet. "Bedroom. Now." Jack stood, his knees popping, and dragged Ethan the rest of the way down the hall. Their trail of clothes stretched from the stairs to the bedroom door as Jack tore his undershirt off and Ethan stripped out of his boxers.

Ethan grabbed Jack, kissing him again, his hands slipping through Jack's hair, cupping the back of his head. Jack seemed to touch him everywhere, fingers dancing over his ribs before stroking down his arms, before cupping his ass and squeezing. Ethan stumbled to the bed, walking backward. The backs of his knees hit the mattress, and Jack gently pushed him down.

And then Jack was on top of him, his warm body covering Ethan's, from their near frantic kisses to their curling toes. Ethan's legs wrapped around Jack's, and his hands raced up and down Jack's back, gripping muscles as he arched and writhed against Jack's body. Jack groaned and thrust against him, their cocks sliding together as he kissed Ethan breathless.

It had been too long for them to make it last. Ethan was too strung out on nerves and anticipation. He came embarrassingly fast, shuddering beneath Jack as Jack pressed an openmouthed kiss to his temple, his ear, and breathed his name. A few moments later, Jack's come seared his belly as Jack's hands threaded through his hair, holding tight as he stared into Ethan's eyes and rode the final crest of his orgasm.

Ethan's arms wound around Jack as he collapsed, pillowing his head on Ethan's chest. He pressed a kiss to the top of Jack's head, smelling his hair, and smiled. "Missed you," he whispered.

Jack's fingers made patterns on Ethan's skin, through his chest hair, tracing the line of his pec and the taut peak of his nipple. "Missed you every single minute."

His throat squeezed shut at that, and his hands stroked up and down Jack's back. He kissed Jack's hair again and looped one of his legs around Jack's. The exhaustion of the week, the peaceful stillness of the Residence, and the serenity of being in Jack's arms again conspired against him, and Ethan's eyelids drooped, falling closed.

As he drifted off, he caught the faint sounds of Jack snoring, and he pressed one last kiss to Jack's mussed dirty-blond hair.

Ethan woke first, before the sun was up. In the darkness of Jack's bedroom, Ethan's gaze roamed over his lover. They hadn't moved much through the night, sleeping diagonally across the large bed and facing each other. Jack's expression had smoothed out in sleep, his laugh lines softer. The curve of his cheek caught a beam of muted light through the window. Ethan curled closer, burying his nose in Jack's hair, holding Jack, letting his mind go blank as his hands caressed Jack's skin, the curves of his muscles, the smooth planes of his back.

Jack's eyes flickered as the sun rose. He smiled before they opened, and he rolled into Ethan's chest, pressing a kiss to his collarbone. "Waking up on Saturday morning with you here is one of my most favorite things."

"Are you hungry? I can make you breakfast." Ethan kissed his temple, rubbing Jack's arms.

"Later. I don't want you to leave." Jack tilted his head up, and his lips found Ethan's.

They traded slow kisses and sleepy grins, their warm bodies tangled together. Ethan's cock, half-hard already, stiffened.

Jack grinned. He rocked against Ethan's thigh until Ethan rolled him over and slid down his body, pressing kisses to his ribs and his hips before he swallowed Jack deep. Shuddering, Jack ran his fingers through Ethan's hair as Ethan's fingers traced ticklish patterns into the soft skin of his thighs.

Ethan reached for the lube and a condom, already out on the bedside table, and pulled them to the bed. Jack's eyes blazed, and he sat up on his elbows as Ethan popped the top off the lube.

Ethan kneeled between Jack's legs and poured some lube onto his fingers.

Jack stroked his cock, mouth open, breathing hard.

Reaching behind himself, Ethan rubbed his fingers over his asshole, slicking and stretching his entrance. His lips parted. He held Jack's burning stare.

"C'mere," Jack whispered. "Let me blow you while you're—"

Flushing, Ethan clambered up the mattress as Jack propped a pillow behind his head. Jack's hands steadied Ethan's hips, as he kissed the head of Ethan's swollen cock before slowly sucking him into his mouth.

Ethan worked quickly, more lube and more fingers, groaning through clenched teeth as he tried not to buck into Jack's hot lips. "Ready," he grunted. "Ready for you."

Jack fumbled for the condom packet. The wrapper crinkled as he tore it open, still sucking on Ethan, and he rolled it over his cock behind Ethan's back. Ethan passed him the lube. The sound of him slicking his condom-covered cock shivered up Ethan's spine.

Biting his lip again, Jack watched wide-eyed as Ethan scooted back on Jack's lap until Jack's cock pressed against him. Ethan rose, fit them together, and sank down slowly.

Jack stared, mouth open, cheeks flushed, hands gripping Ethan's thighs and nails digging into his skin. Inch by inch, Ethan worked himself down as Jack speared him. The stretch, the feeling of Jack entering his body, writhed just beneath his skin, a liquid heat that slithered through him. His eyes rolled back, his mouth dropping open.

Jack whimpered, shuddering when Ethan bottomed out, impaled on his cock.

They moved slowly at first, Ethan rocking on Jack's lap and stroking his chest, running his fingers over Jack's skin until he laced their fingers together and pushed Jack's hands over his head. He moved deeper, riding Jack's cock in long, slow movements, up and down, as Jack shivered and whispered his name, staring into his eyes.

Eventually, Ethan picked up the pace, driving down on Jack faster, harder, curling over Jack, their foreheads pressed together, sweat pricking at their skin. Jack reached for Ethan, cupping his hands around the back of his neck as he gasped. Ethan braced one hand on the headboard and stroked his cock furiously with the other.

"I'm close," Jack breathed. "You're too hot. Too beautiful. Ethan—" He groaned, his eyes rolling back, but they snapped back to Ethan's face, staring.

"God, me too." Ethan shuddered, coiled lust tight in his gut. "Shit. *Shit*, Jack. Come with me. Come—"

Jack lunged, driving into Ethan as he tugged at Ethan's neck, pressing their lips together and kissing him with wide-open eyes as Ethan's orgasm tore through his body. He moaned into Jack's kiss, come splattering Jack's chest as his whole body clenched and quivered. Jack gasped, and his hips snapped up, pressed deep into Ethan as his hands cupped Ethan's cheeks, and his trembling lips kissed Ethan breathless.

They kissed until Jack slipped from Ethan's body. Jack palmed the condom off and let it drop to the floor before wiping his chest clean with a towel hidden by the bed. Ethan pitched sideways, nuzzling Jack's neck, and they dozed off holding hands, foreheads pressed together.

5

Washington DC

Rumbling stomachs forced them to rise around noon. Hair sticking every which way, they padded to the kitchen and made sandwiches together just in their boxers, trading kisses and wrapping their arms around each other's waists. Ethan blended smoothies for them, and they sat in the West Sitting Hall and fed each other slowly.

Jack brought out his notes for the UN, the Joint Chiefs' proposals, and President Puchkov's alliance, and they spread everything out on the couches and tables as they talked it all through. Ethan laughed as Jack, shirtless, made stacks of the Joint Chiefs' proposals for military operations, counting them off one by one. Later, he sat next to him on the couch and rubbed Jack's feet while he listened to Jack speculate on President Puchkov's eccentricities. They moved to the combat plans next, and Jack turned pensive.

"I want your opinion, Ethan. What would be best for the troops on the ground? You've been there. Done this before." Jack swallowed, his Adam's apple rising and falling, as he sat with his elbows braced on his knees. "I want to bring everyone home."

It was an impossible ask, but Ethan knew where Jack's desire came from: a folded flag and a white headstone in Arlington with his wife's name etched into the marble.

They talked until the sky turned dark and the lights in the Residence winked on around them. Ethan held out his hand for Jack and led him to the shower. He washed Jack slowly as Jack tipped his head back and closed his eyes. Jack let Ethan dry his hair, rubbing the towel over his head as he scrunched up his nose and laughed at himself in the mirror.

Jeans and long-sleeve pullovers later, they headed down from the Residence. Ethan sheepishly collected their trail of clothes first, though. From the landing at the middle of the stairs, anyone could have seen the start of the trail. How many of his fellow agents had chuckled at the display?

Jack threaded his fingers through Ethan's as they came down the stairs. Daniels and Beech appeared in the Cross Hall, arriving from the West Wing. "Saw you on the monitors." Daniels grinned. "Coming down for air?"

Ethan blushed as Jack spoke. "I'd like a tour of the Christmas decorations." He squeezed Ethan's hand. "I waited for you so we could do it together."

Ethan's heart burst.

Daniels called out over the radio, "Vigilant and Reichenbach about to tour the decorations. Be advised."

They started in the Cross Hall, admiring the garlands and wreaths strung overhead. Bulbs in every color glittered from the garlands, along with crushed velvet bows. Poinsettias clustered around the columns and the foot of the Grand Staircase, and a red-and-gold ribbon swirled under the bannister, heading up the stairs.

At one end of the Cross Hall, a stately evergreen stood tall, overlooking the presidential portraits. Gold stars hung from the thick boughs, and plush red, white, and blue ribbons twirled around the tree.

"This is the Armed Forces tree," Ethan said softly, squeezing Jack's hand. "A gold star for—"

Jack nodded, gripping his hand too-tight. His eyes pinched, but he stared at the tree as Ethan held his hand. "The names are on the stars," Ethan whispered. "Her name is up there."

Jack closed his eyes. He pressed a long kiss to the back of Ethan's hand, breathed in, and then turned away. "What's next?"

Ethan led him down the hall, pointing out the oversized snowflakes hanging in between the garlands. Glittering and suspended almost in midair, they twirled slowly, winking in the soft light of the hall. "Fifty-six snowflakes," he said. "One for every state and territory."

From room to room they went, from the China Room, and its army of snowmen and a flocked tree trimmed with glittering lights, to the Library, where winter forest creatures played on the bookshelves and a rustic woodland theme seemed to sweep the room away. Thick velvet and holly berries twined with the evergreen garlands, and a squat pine sat in the center of the room, bedecked with antique ornaments. The fire crackled, and oversized stockings hung from the mantel, cradled by delicate snow bunnies and porcelain reindeer.

Secret Service agents had shown up in twos and threes, filing into the rooms and watching Jack and Ethan. They were relaxed and casual, and Ethan's heart warmed in the Blue Room when he figured out what they were all doing.

"During the holidays, the Secret Service helps out with the tours," he said, leaning close to Jack. "We all really like it, actually. People are always nice, and it's the only time visitors can take pictures. We stand post in the different rooms and give a little presentation. Tell them what's there and the history of the room. The decorations." He nodded to the agents hanging out by the tree. "Looks like they're putting on a private tour for you."

Jack beamed and headed for the agents. Beech, Caldwell, Hawkins, and Hanier stood off to one side next to the official White House Christmas tree. They smiled at Jack, shook his hand, and then Jack was off, asking question after question about the tree—decked out in white ornaments, white lights, and white satin ribbon—and the decorations around the room—golden baubles and snowflakes that hung in the windows overlooking the South Lawn. Beyond, the Washington Monument rose into the night sky, lit up for the world.

Daniels sidled up to Ethan, his hands in his pockets and chuckling at Jack posing for pictures with the Secret Service agents in front of the tree. Each agent had to stand for two pictures—one for their camera and a selfie on Jack's.

"Thanks." Ethan met Daniels's bright gaze. "This will mean a lot to him."

Daniels clapped him on the back. "Means a lot to us, too. Having you both here." He squeezed Ethan's shoulder. "It's not the same without you."

What could he say to that? Ethan looked away, squinting, but smiled when Jack headed back. "It's a peace tree." Jack whistled, looking the tree up and down. "Did you know it is eighteen feet and two inches tall?"

"Eighteen two?" Ethan took his hand. "It was seventeen eleven and half last year."

"We're supposed to go to the Red Room next." Jack grinned. "I was promised a good story there."

Ethan laughed and led Jack out into the hall. "This one is all on Scott. And he's not even here to protest."

They made their way into the Red Room, once a salon to first ladies in the 1800s. Ruby walls and rich-red furnishings gave the room its name, and cranberries were the decoration of choice. Three delicate Christmas trees stood in an arc, circled with cranberry garlands, pomegranates, and bright-red apples. Painted cardinals perched on branches and evergreen boughs were draped along the walls, twinkling with sparkling lights.

Miniature evergreen trees and topiaries made from cranberries sat on the tables in between flickering candles and silver sculptures of snowmen and reindeer.

"So," Daniels said slowly. "No joke, Agent Collard once tried to eat his way through this room."

The other agents laughed as Jack's jaw dropped. "He's lucky this is all edible."

"It was the year everyone made a big deal about being organic. I don't know what was going on with him. Maybe he was hungover, or—" Ethan shook his head. "But he was starving, and in between every tour, he'd start munching on the cranberries. Swiped a bunch of apples. At the end of his shift, he had to smuggle out this urn he'd stuffed his fruit cores into."

"The urn is still down in Horsepower," Hawkins called out. "Hoffer put it up on the main desk."

41

"Hoffer was the lead before me." Ethan's arm snaked around Jack's waist. "He retired, and I got the job." His lips thinned, and Jack's hand fell to his, holding it in place on his hip. He'd gotten *the* job, the best position in the Secret Service, and had lost it in less than a year.

"He tried to turn the cranberry trees so no one could see the eaten parts." Daniels shook his head, laughing along with the other agents. "You could hear the screeching all the way in Virginia when the florist discovered the wreckage."

"Did she figure out who did it?" Jack's eyes twinkled.

Ethan, Daniels, and all the agents shook their heads. "We kept that one in the ranks." Daniels winked. "You're an honorary agent now, I guess, Mr. President."

Jack grinned, and they all filed out, Jack shaking his head and chuckling. They moved down the Cross Hall again, beneath the glittering chandeliers and the softly spinning snowflakes. Jack kept his fingers laced with Ethan's, their footsteps muffled in the thick red carpet running the length of the hall.

"This next room—" Ethan's throat tightened. "This was my room. I held post here for years during the holidays. It's the best."

Jack squeezed his hand.

And then the agents ahead pushed open the heavy wooden doors to the East Room, the largest room in the White House, where all the balls and receptions took place. Ethan's breath caught, Jack's jaw dropped, and even Daniels whistled as the group wandered in.

Iridescent and gold icicles hung from the ceiling, alongside shining globes and crystal snowflakes. Champagne, winter-white, and silver fabric draped the walls, sweeping along the crown molding and tumbling to the floor. Wreaths trimmed in golden ribbon hung on the walls. Four Christmas trees, smaller than the official tree, but not by much, lined the back wall between the windows, covered in dazzling icicles, pearl garlands, vintage jewels and gemstones, and gold and snow-white orbs. Over the fireplace, an overlarge mirror had been decked in garlands and champagne ribbons, and golden stockings hung from silver snowflake hangers. "President of the

United States" had been stitched on one of the stockings, and next to it, "Vice President of the United States."

Ethan's heart did a flip-flop, his chest tightening. "They have other stockings," he said softly. "Usually there are ones for the First Family up there, too."

Jack's thumb brushed over Ethan's bruised and scabbed knuckles. "These stockings are nice." He leaned into Ethan. "But we'll have our own upstairs. Yours will be right next to mine. Where it should be."

He wanted to kiss Jack, but there were agents with them. Other than when Ethan had appeared back from the dead, they were circumspect in their public displays of affection. Another piece of their puzzle—trying to keep media attention away from them, away from their lives.

Though, there were no cameras in the room, no media; just him and Jack and agents who had been Ethan's friends and comrades for years.

But still… he held back.

"Tell me about what you did here." Jack tugged him around the room, inspecting everything, listening as Ethan relayed story after story of standing post in the East Room. From his first holiday season twelve years ago to the last, a year before he joined Jack's campaign. Little kids he remembered awed by the decorations, shyly waving at him from behind their parents' legs. Endless pictures he took of tourists in front of the trees and the fireplace, trying to get people to laugh when he took their picture by calling out something ridiculous instead of "cheese."

"All the holiday parties are in here, too. The big Christmas Ball. All the others." He frowned, and Daniels made his way over. "Levi, how many photo lines is Jack doing this year?"

Daniels whistled. "Oh, way, way less. Only two, actually. The big Christmas Ball and the Hanukkah Festival of Lights. The rest are parties without photo lines, and even those are way down."

"Good."

Jack's eyes darted from Daniels to Ethan, and his eyebrows quirked up.

"Photo lines are hard on everyone, but especially the president. You stand here—" Ethan pointed in front of one of the trees, next to the fireplace. "And you shake hands and take a photo with every one of your guests. It takes hours. And you'll get the weirdest people there. People who have just vilified you. They'll stand in line and take a photo with you at Christmas like nothing is wrong." Ethan shook his head. "The congressman who led the impeachment against your predecessor? He came here for a Christmas photo."

"Yeah, Mr. President, between your travel schedule, your weekends already being booked, and the sensitivity of everything, your chief of staff pulled out all but ten Christmas parties at the White House." Daniels ran his hand over his mouth, exhaling. "It's still a lot. You are only scheduled for the two photo lines, Mr. President, and the other eight... Well, you're actually out of town for three of them. VPOTUS will take those."

Jack's eyebrows had continued to climb, almost all the way off his forehead. "Lawrence cancelled holiday parties because of the sensitivity of the situation?" His eyes flicked to Ethan. "You're *not* talking about Ethan and I, right?"

Daniels shook his head quickly. "No, Mr. President. The upcoming combat operations. Going to war. Never looks good to celebrate before a war."

Jack exhaled, but nodded. "I agree. But we also can't let go of traditions that unite and define us. That give us hope."

"This is a good balance, Mr. President. This time of the year gets hectic, and you're already traveling a lot. You don't need a ton of appearances on top of that. You'll run yourself down."

Ethan stood at Jack's side, listening to Daniels gently counsel Jack into agreement. It was part of the Secret Service job, guiding the president at times to the right decision for his safety and security. And sanity. "The Christmas Ball is great." He rested his hand on Jack's lower back. "You'll love it."

"Will you be there?" Bright hope shone from Jack's gaze.

Ethan looked to Daniels.

"It's two days before Christmas."

The day he arrived for his Christmas vacation. No matter what Shepherd said, Ethan wasn't the kind of guy to just blow off his job, his responsibilities, or the oath he took when he became a Special Agent. He had his vacation days and he was sticking to them, no matter that he wanted more with Jack. "I will be. I'll get in that day."

Jack pressed a kiss to Ethan's cheek. "Hey, let's get a photo in front of the tree."

They went for the big tree next to the fireplace, and Daniels snapped pictures on his and Jack's phones, first of everyone gathered together and then of just Jack and Ethan, arms wrapped around each other's waists, smiling for the camera. The rest of the agents clustered behind Daniels, watching and grinning.

"C'mon, Ethan. Act like you like the guy a little bit. Give him a kiss!"

The agents whistled and cheered, laughing as Jack's ears flushed a ruby red. But he turned to Ethan and smiled, a question in his eyes.

It was all on Ethan.

They tried to be circumspect everywhere, tried to nip the media frenzy in the bud, but this was their home. These were men who Ethan had served next to for years, men he considered friends, and who were cheering them on, literally and in every other way imaginable. Did he need to hold back in front of such support?

He cupped Jack's cheek, his thumb stroking Jack's warm skin, and leaned in, capturing his lips in a slow, heated kiss. Jack smiled against him, moaned softly, and slid his fingers through Ethan's hair as Daniels and the rest of the agents catcalled and clapped.

"Whoa, whoa!" Daniels kept taking pictures, practically a hundred of them kissing in front of the tree. "Do we need to vacate? Give us a minute to give you the room, sir!"

And then Jack was laughing, turning away from Ethan with crimson cheeks, but he gripped Ethan tight, clinging to his shoulders. Ethan held his waist, and they shared a lingering look as the agents started to file out.

Daniels made his way back to their side, handing Jack his phone. "Ready to head home? Or want to hang for a bit?"

Jack laced his hand through Ethan's and brought it to his lips. "Home."

"Will you tell me what happened?"

Jack traced the scabs and bruises on Ethan's knuckles, almost but not quite healed from when he'd tried to murder the boxing bag in the Des Moines field office gym.

They were in the Residence's kitchen, leaning against the counter, sharing a beer and laughing at the pictures Daniels had taken on Jack's phone. Unbeknownst to them, Daniels had flipped the camera at one point and the agents behind him had all smiled for a group selfie.

Ethan chugged for a moment, not looking at Jack. "I was frustrated." His voice was low, and it ground through his throat.

Jack waited.

He finished the beer and rolled the bottle back and forth in his hands. Sighed. Set the bottle on the counter behind him and closed his eyes. "You know the case I was working on? The one I told you about?"

"The counterfeiting ring. The one you just made the arrests on?"

"I… had to give it up. Transfer it to another agent. I'm not allowed to run any investigations on my own anymore."

Jack frowned, a deep line furrowing between his eyebrows.

"I still build the cases, and I'm still investigating… a little. But I have to turn everything over to Agent Becker." He snorted. "Blake Becker was twelve years old when I started in the Secret Service. Twelve."

"Why? Is this punishment?"

"It's containment." Chewing his lip, Ethan scuffed at the floor with the toe of his shoe. Rubber squeaked on tile. "If I were to lead a case that went all the way to court, my whole history can be brought up. My character. The kinds of decisions I've made." He couldn't look at Jack, not with this. "Any case I manage would be destroyed in court."

Silence.

"I'm sorry," Jack breathed.

"Not your fault."

Ethan could feel the burn of Jack's gaze on his profile. "It's not yours either."

It was Ethan's turn to stay silent.

"I made my choices—" he finally started.

"*We* made *our* choices."

"And I knew the price when I made them." Finally, he turned to Jack. There was pain in Jack's eyes, frustration and anger. "I knew this would be the price I had to pay. Losing this." He jerked his chin, trying to encompass the whole of the White House. "Losing privileges. Losing credibility."

Exhaling hard, Jack leaned on the counter, his forearms on the marble. His eyes flashed, raw anger surging and scaring away the pain. "You shouldn't lose any credibility. You're a hero, damn it. You saved everyone." Jack swallowed. "I mean that. *Everyone.*"

Ethan turned and shouldered up to him. "I'm okay. I have what's important." He nudged him and tried to smile. "It's all worth it for me because I get to come here and do this." He leaned in, dropping a kiss to the corner of Jack's lips.

Jack didn't seem ready to let it go. He frowned. "Your boss can't help at all? I thought the Secret Service was close. You would do anything for your guys. Hell, you *did* do everything for them. You and Agent Collard saved so many lives when you retook the White House."

Snorting, Ethan shook his head. "No. Shepherd would rather see me bounced out of the Secret Service. If he could take my badge and gun, he would."

That didn't help. Jack's anger surged back. Ethan could feel it thrumming through Jack's body, tightening his muscles.

Jack shoved back from the counter and went for the fridge, pulling out another bottle of beer. His gaze, though, landed on

Ethan's scabbed knuckles, and all the fight seemed to flee out of him. "So," he said, coming back to Ethan's side. His fingers traced over Ethan's battered knuckles again. "What happened?"

"Beat a punching bag a few hundred times." Ethan tried to smile, tried to turn it into a joke, but it came out sad.

"Call me instead? I'll always listen."

This time, Ethan really did smile. It was small and soft, but it was there. "Okay."

"And... is there anything I can do?" Earnestness had replaced the anger in Jack's gaze.

"People already think I get special treatment." He leaned over, kissing Jack's cheek. "I don't think getting you involved will put that rumor to bed." Jack grumbled but drank his beer.

And then he turned back to Ethan, a sly grin curling his lips. "I know this one agency, though. Real workhorses. You may have heard of them. Called the IRS."

Ethan laughed out loud, his head tipping back. "No."

"What? Surprise audits going ten years back for all the people who have even looked sideways at you. Everyone will be too busy to bother you anymore!"

He kept laughing, pulling Jack to him and burying his face in Jack's hair. "It would be too many people to audit. You'd need more IRS agents."

"Done. For you? Done."

Ethan pressed kisses to Jack's ear, light and delicate. "I'm okay, Jack," he said softly. "Really. This—" Smiling, he squeezed Jack's shoulders. Pressed his forehead to Jack's. "This is what matters most to me. Right here."

They went to bed after that, lounging naked in Jack's bed, talking. Jack wanted to hear everything about Iowa. About Shepherd, about Blake Becker. About the case he'd built, and how he'd had to give it all away. Jack's eyes were full of sadness as they lay face-to-face on the pillows, talking softly with the lights off. Ethan had one leg hitched between Jack's and one hand tangled in Jack's hair, his thumb stroking Jack's temple.

Fear lingered in the edges of Jack's eyes, in the shine of his gaze in the moonlight.

"I don't regret it," Ethan whispered. "I'm happy with you."

Jack smiled and curled closer, and they fell asleep wrapped around each other and holding hands.

6

"Ethan!"

Ethan bolted upright, blood pounding through his chest, his arms, his adrenaline racing and making his hands shake. Darkness pressed in on all sides, and he searched for Jack, tearing at the bedsheets. What was happening? Where was the threat? He had to get Jack, get him to safety—

Jack grasped his hand, his arm, and tugged him close, shuddering and gasping and clinging to Ethan in a cold sweat. His fingernails bit into Ethan's shoulder as he clung to him, tried to climb his skin.

Ethan's adrenaline petered away, leaving him cold and drifting, listless in the bed as he wrapped his arms around Jack. Jack was trembling, shivering, and trying to crawl into Ethan's lap. "Jack?" He nuzzled his lover's sweaty forehead, pressed kisses to his eyelids. "Jack, what's wrong?"

Jack fought for words, clinging to Ethan and working to calm his breathing. The sheets were tangled between them, tied around Jack's waist almost in a knot. "Ethan," he exhaled, his nails still digging into Ethan's shoulders. "Ethan… *God*, it was so real…"

"What was?" Ethan kissed Jack's hairline. Stroked his back.

"Ethiopia. Except this time, you were dead. Really dead. I was in the street, over your body, and your blood was *everywhere*—"

"Shhhh." He pulled him fully onto his lap. Jack went, molding himself to Ethan's chest as Ethan leaned back against the headboard and ran his hands up and down Jack's trembling arms and over his clammy back. "I'm not dead, Jack. I'm right here."

"I was holding you when you died." Jack's voice was small, almost a whisper. "I wanted to tell you I loved you, but—" And then he couldn't speak. He closed his eyes and rested his cheek on Ethan's shoulder.

Ethan held him until the trembling stopped, until Jack's breathing leveled out, and then held him some more, his hands caressing every inch of Jack's back, his shoulders, and his arms. Finally, he slipped his fingers into the short strands of dirty-blond hair at the base of his neck. "I'm here, Jack," he murmured. "I'm here with you. I'm with you all the way."

"I'm sorry," Jack finally grunted. He pushed back, sitting up, but didn't meet Ethan's gaze. "I'm sorry for waking you."

"Hey." Ethan cupped Jack's cheek, drawing his gaze up. "I will always wake up to be with you. Always."

Jack tried to smile. He failed.

"Nightmare?"

His eyes slid away. "They're not every night."

"Which means they're more than just tonight." Ethan's other hand joined the first, cradling Jack's face before he leaned in and kissed him. "Why didn't you say anything?"

Jack looked down. He picked at the sheet, at a loose thread. "I didn't... I didn't go through what you went through. Why am I having nightmares? It's stupid. I'm—" He clamped his mouth shut.

"You were held hostage, Jack. Betrayed by your friend. They strapped a nuke to you. If you didn't have nightmares, I'd be worried."

"I don't have nightmares about that. You were there. You saved me. Us." Finally, Jack looked up. "I only have nightmares about losing you."

What could he say to that? Guilt flooded his heart, sliding down his insides. Jack had enough to worry about without having nightmares about him. He shouldn't have been captured. Shouldn't have ever brought Jack to Ethiopia and sent Jack down this twisted path of dark fears.

"How often?" he whispered.

Jack shrugged. "Sometimes a couple nights a week. Sometimes I can go almost two weeks before it happens again."

"What do you do when..."

"I get up. Read. I've got a thousand briefing papers I need to read. A thousand different memos. I can always find something to do." Jack was trying to smile, but it didn't reach his eyes.

"Call me next time? If I can't be here to hold you, then I want to be there to talk to you."

"It's the middle of the night—"

"I always have my phone right next to my pillow. Just in case you call." Ethan kissed each of Jack's knuckles, his lips lingering on his skin. "I want to be there for you, Jack. For everything. Even when I can't be right here to hold you like this. I still want to do everything that I can."

Nodding, Jack finally managed a tiny smile. "Okay," he breathed.

They kissed slowly and lay down again, and Jack passed out with his head pillowed on Ethan's chest, his ear over Ethan's heart.

In the morning, they made love again, soft and sweet, grinding slowly as they kissed and kissed and kissed, until they came pressed tight together, legs interlocked, smiles on their faces.

After lounging naked, Ethan rose with a kiss and made Jack breakfast in bed, bringing back a tray of eggs, French toast, sausage, orange juice, and coffee. Jack shared bites with Ethan, feeding him as they held hands and traded kisses.

Jack's cell phone rang when they were finished, and Jack heaved a heavy sigh before he answered. He squeezed Ethan's hand, though, and Ethan sat back against the headboard as Jack answered.

"Hello, Mom."

Ethan couldn't hear Jack's mom, but he watched Jack close his eyes and then pinch the bridge of his nose. "I know, Mom, I know. But I really want you to hear me on this. I know you promised you'd spend my first Christmas in the White House with me. But, this year, it's just going to be me and Ethan."

Jack squeezed Ethan's hand again, smiling.

"That's why I came to see you for Thanksgiving. It's our first Christmas together, Mom." He sighed, tipping his head back. "Yes, Mom, you're right. He was with me last year over Christmas, but that doesn't count. We weren't together. This is our first Christmas *together*. As a couple."

Jack's mom got quiet on her end, but Jack was still smiling. Ethan watched the laugh lines deepen at the corners of his eyes and the way his shoulders relaxed. "Yeah, I'm hoping there are a lot more Christmases together too," he said, rubbing his thumb over Ethan's palm. "And yes, we will all celebrate together in the future. But this one? It's going to be his and mine. Just the two of us." A pause. "Thanks, Mom. Tell Dad I said hi. Love you too."

He tossed the phone on the nightstand and gave Ethan a rueful grin. "She's desperate to meet you."

"Do you want your family to come here? I know you guys are close."

"No." Jack smiled, lying down and resting his head in Ethan's lap. "We are close. But I meant what I said. I want this to be our time. Just us. Maybe next year we can all get together."

Next year. Jack had already tossed out next Thanksgiving Day plans, saying he wanted Ethan with him. And now Christmas plans with his family. Ethan was all in, one hundred percent committed, but a lingering fear squatted in the darkness of his heart. How long would Jack keep this up? Until the novelty wore off? Until he didn't like the media hounding him? When would that happen?

Never, Ethan hoped. Never, ever.

"What about your family?" Jack rolled over, resting his cheek on Ethan's thigh. "What are they doing?"

Ethan brushed Jack's hair off his forehead and smiled. "Dad passed away. Cancer got him ten years ago. He was a two-packs-a-day smoker my whole life."

"I'm sorry."

"It's all right. We were close, and I was able to get out there before he died. We had our goodbyes." He'd driven his dad up into the forest, into the mountains, and they'd sat on the tailgate of his dad's pickup and fished by the lake. Drunk beers and watched the Wyoming sun set, and then rested around a crackling campfire. His dad had been frail and he huddled inside a jean jacket that seemed almost like a muumuu, and then under a thick blanket as the sun wore down the day, but he'd smiled through it all.

"Be happy, son," his dad had said. *"That's all I ever wanted for you. Be happy."*

At the time, he had been, and he told his dad so. His dad just beamed at him, content to the marrow of his bones as he watched the fire settle and the logs shift beneath the stars.

A few days later, his dad passed in his sleep, and Ethan scattered his ashes in those same woods.

Jack listened as Ethan relayed their final days. When he was done, Jack pressed a kiss to his palm. He didn't say anything for a long moment. "Your mom?"

"Never knew her. She took off sometime after I was born. It was just Dad and me and our little trailer. He was a farmhand, and I'd hang around him and help out when I wasn't in school. Pick fruit on the farms over summer. Go with him in the mornings to help in the barn. We didn't have much, but we had enough. Dad wanted me to go to college, and he would buy me books whenever he had extra cash. Enlisting in the Army was my ticket to more opportunity. From the Army, I went to the Secret Service." Ethan leaned over. Jack and kissed him. "What about you?"

Jack shrugged. "Nothing that interesting. Dad was a corporate lawyer. Mom stayed with me. Little League and piano lessons. Boy Scouts and football. We were good, but Dad was busy a lot. We got really close after Leslie died, though." Jack smiled, sad on the edges. "They were amazing."

"I'm glad you had them."

And then it was Sunday afternoon, and the reality of Ethan leaving in several hours began to set in. Just like every Sunday, they grew quieter, held each other longer. Ethan lay on the couch in Jack's study, Jack stretched out on top of him as Ethan breathed in the scent of his hair. Kissed his head and stroked his back. Football droned on the TV, but Ethan couldn't remember the score.

"You fly to New York on Thursday, right?" he murmured into Jack's scalp.

"I meet with Puchkov that night. Address the Security Council on Friday. My advisors are saying they expect the deliberations to go into Saturday, with a vote late Saturday or even Sunday."

They were losing the next weekend, too, thanks to Jack's pitch at the UN. "You're going to do great."

"Will you help me with my speech this week? Over Skype?"

"Of course."

Jack swallowed, and Ethan felt it through the tight press of their bodies. "I won't see you again until you come back for Christmas?"

"Yeah." Ethan had rearranged the days so that he'd miss a weekend, but be back in DC for longer over the holiday. "On the twenty-third. Be here until Sunday."

"Five days." Pushing up, Jack grinned, his mussed hair standing every which way. "Five days with you here. It will be..." His grin turned sly. "Like Christmas!"

Ethan laughed, and he kissed him until he thought his heart would burst.

Scott took him back to the airport every Sunday night, picking him up in the private underground entrance to the Residence in an unmarked SUV. Agents were scattered around the garage, doing their best to give them both some privacy. Unlike yesterday, no one was smiling.

The goodbye was always excruciating.

Ethan and Jack held each other while Scott loaded Ethan's duffel and made himself scarce at the rear of the SUV.

"Knock 'em dead at the UN." Ethan kissed Jack's nose. "You'll be amazing. I know you will."

"Good luck with your case." Jack tugged on Ethan's scarf. "*Your* case. I don't care that an infant is the case agent. It's yours. You did the work."

"Call me when you need me." Leaning in, Ethan pressed his forehead to Jack's, staring into his eyes.

Jack nodded. "You too, okay?"

"Okay."

And then they kissed until Scott coughed to get their attention. Ethan reluctantly broke away. He bit his lip, caressed Jack's cheeks with his gloved thumbs, and kissed Jack's forehead again as Jack's hands refused to let go of his thick trench coat.

"Sixteen days until I see you again," Jack whispered, kissing Ethan one last time.

Ethan groaned. "That's way too long." Ethan stole another kiss.

"We gotta go." Scott always sounded like he was telling them their mothers had died, interrupting as quietly as he could with the terrible news. "We're running behind as it is, and the snow's coming in again."

Finally, Jack stepped back, releasing Ethan. Ethan headed for the SUV. As they pulled out, he watched Jack in the rearview mirror until they turned out and he couldn't see him any longer. Behind them, Jack crossed his arms, rubbed his hands over his sleeves, and shivered in the freezing underground garage. But he waited and watched Ethan and Scott pull away, all the way out of the garage, every time.

The ride was always silent. There was nothing to say after that, and he and Scott kept up through text and the occasional phone call anyway. Just having Scott in the car with him was enough, sitting next to him in the darkness as the lights of DC smeared against the windshield and fell over his face.

At the airport, Ethan shouldered through a gaggle of reporters, all vying for a picture, and escaped into the terminal. Within minutes, his federal shadow appeared, standing three spots behind him in line at the coffee shop. Ethan paid for his coffee and then paid for his shadow's.

His shadow toasted him with his paper cup after taking up position on his right, ninety degrees off, inside twenty yards, leaning against a wall and trying to look nonchalant.

They boarded forty-five minutes later, Ethan collapsing into his first-class seat with a sigh. His phone buzzed.

A text from Jack. A single sad face emoji.

Ethan sent back the one with a tear slipping free. *[Miss you already.]*

Gotta get working on that time machine.

[I love you.]

The flight attendants dimmed the lights and shut the doors, and the announcement came on about turning off all cell phones. Sighing, Ethan hit the power button.

I love you so much, Ethan.

Jack's text flashed before the power cut out, and his heart leaped into his throat as his eyes watered and his lungs burned. The agony of leaving Jack was searingly intense, almost as intense as the love Ethan felt for him.

But this was the price that had to be paid. He'd known the cost. He'd always known it would turn out this way.

7

Des Moines, Iowa

Agent Blake Becker swallowed hard, his face pale, as the medical examiner gripped the edge of the white sheet covering the body.

Ethan eyed him, holding out his hand to still the medical examiner. "You ever seen a dead body before?" He kept his voice low, turning so he was speaking just into Becker's ear.

Becker shook his head, fast shakes, his eyes never leaving the lump beneath the sheet. "Just the slides from that one course in training."

Forensics for Special Agents. How to not fuck up a crime scene until the real techs got on deck. For Special Agents like Becker, running financial crimes investigations, the chances of encountering a dead body were scarce to laughable. Ethan, running on the other side of the Secret Service—protecting the president—had a daily realistic possibility of having to shoot someone—or multiple someones—dead. And he had.

A gulf of experience separated him and his case agent, a man he was supposed to be working under.

"It's going to be overwhelming. Try to focus on areas. Don't get lost in the whole body. Did you put your menthol on?"

Becker nodded. He closed his eyes and took a deep breath.

Ethan pulled his hand back. The medical examiner glanced between them and flicked back the sheet, exposing the dead woman lying on the refrigerated steel rack. "She was found Saturday morning dumped off I-35," the medical examiner grunted. "Time of death... best estimate is sometime late Thursday or early Friday morning."

Next to Ethan, Becker shuddered, turning away from the corpse, his hand covering his mouth as he coughed.

The isolation had done its job. She'd been left in the snow for over twenty-four hours, and parts of her body had frozen black with decay. Her skin had pulled taut, stretched across her pale face as if she were screaming, crying out in agony. Blood pooling on her right side turned the parts of her skin not frozen a rotten black into a deep emerald and aubergine. Dependent lividity. She'd been dumped on her right, and her blood had followed gravity's natural pull.

Her wrists had been bound. Angry ligature marks broke the skin, bloody scabs flaking free. Her abdomen had been stabbed fourteen times, slices and tears shredding her midsection into thin filets of flesh. One large Y-incision went from her collarbones to her pubic bone, the marks of her autopsy. Her organs were gone, off for analysis, but the medical examiner had stitched her back up, giant black Frankenstein stitches running up her skin.

Ethan dragged in a deep breath through his nose, letting the menthol he'd smeared over his lip fill his lungs, tingling his body. It centered him, put his feet squarely back on the ground, and took his mind off the grotesqueness before him.

He flipped open the folder of crime scenes photos he'd been given by the Des Moines police officer on his way into the morgue. "She was found with counterfeit bills stuffed in her mouth?"

"Seven counterfeit hundreds." The medical examiner pointed to her open mouth. "Some were shoved deep in her throat. Enough to choke on."

Ethan frowned down at one of the evidence photos: all seven of the bills in a plastic bag. "The blood on the bills. Is that ante- or postmortem?"

"Antemortem. She was alive when they were shoved in."

Becker appeared at Ethan's shoulder, ghost white. "Are we done here?"

"Have you ID'd her yet?" Ethan's gaze roamed over the girl. Late teens. Maybe twenties. Maybe younger. Evidence of a hard life pocked her skin. Track marks on her arms, needle scabs and scars in her veins. Old scars from cigarette burns on her thighs. A softness to her hips that suggested she'd carried a child.

"Unfortunately no. She's still a Jane Doe. Nothing in our system on her prints or her DNA. Whatever she's been doing, she's been under the radar. Until now."

Ethan stared down at her, tracing with his eyes the discoloration on her right cheek, the scrapes on her face, the harsh angle of her jaw. Broken, the report had said. Jaw broken.

"Reichenbach…" Becker strained voice over Ethan's shoulder finally shook him free.

"Yeah. We're done here. Let's go." Nodding his thanks to the medical examiner, Ethan strode out after Becker, pushing through the double swing doors of the basement morgue and thundering up the stairs to the main lobby. Becker took them two at a time, his trench coat flaring behind him, practically running for freedom. He didn't stop at the lobby, just stormed on, shoving open the doors to police headquarters and almost jogging around the side of the building.

Ethan followed and found Becker doubled over, hands braced on his knees, heaving sour yogurt into the dirty snowdrift shoveled off the sidewalk.

He stood at Becker's side, silent, and waited for him to spit and stand.

Becker avoided his gaze. "Got an email. The bills are the same counterfeits from the bust last week. Maybe there's a connection." He tried to shoulder past Ethan.

Ethan grabbed him at the elbow. "It happens to everyone."

Becker's eyes flashed, and for a moment, Ethan thought Becker would shove him away. Then he chuffed out a single laugh, shaking his head. "You shot and killed fourteen guys mid-coup in the Oval Office and then saved the president from a nuke strapped to his chest. I don't think *anything* shakes you, Reichenbach."

He tried to smile, but it was brittle. "Ethiopia did."

Becker frowned. Recognition flooded his gaze. "You were a hostage."

"I mean before. I really thought we wouldn't make it out of there. That Jack would die no matter what I did to try to save him."

"You guys were together then, right?"

He nodded.

"I mean, from what the president said, yeah, but—" Becker shook his head, looking away.

Ethan could tell there was more he wanted to say, more he wanted to ask. The clenching of his jaw, the muscles twitching in his neck.

"Let's go. We've got to work this. Figure out why those counterfeit bills are shoved into some murdered girl's throat. We should question those perps again. See if they can ID her." Becker took off, fast-walking away from Ethan down the salt-strewn sidewalk.

"Hey."

Becker stopped but didn't turn.

"Let's grab lunch first, okay? I'd like to talk through the evidence. Figure out what to ask." Becker needed to level out. Calm his head. Let the adrenaline go.

Becker arched his eyebrows, a tiny smile curling his lips. "Going out to lunch in public with a male agent? You don't think the media wouldn't be all over that? Shepherd's head would explode."

Ethan shrugged. "Maybe we can swing through a drive-through."

Becker tossed him the keys. "You're driving. Pick someplace good."

Doreen took one look at the picture of the murdered girl's face and heaved, vomiting all over the front of her orange prison jumpsuit.

"What the fuck?" She spat vomit to the ground between her shackled legs and slammed her fists on the steel table. "You can't fucking do that!"

Becker stared. "I take it you know this woman?"

Doreen's eyes narrowed to slits. She slammed her fists on the table again. "*Fuck* you!"

"All right." Ethan stepped up, coming out of the corner and resting his hand on Becker's shoulder. "Why don't I take it from here?"

Becker snorted and pushed away from the table, but when he turned his back on Doreen, he sent Ethan a quick wink. "She's all yours," he snapped, shoving the folder of crime scene pics against Ethan's chest. He walked out, slamming the door to the interrogation room behind him.

"Fucking asshole!" Doreen shouted after him. Her dark, stringy hair shivered, ratty ends brushing the top of the table. She plucked at her hair, fingers running over the ends, over and over again.

Ethan sat and pulled out one of the autopsy photos, one showing just the left side of the girl's face. Her jaw was closed with a gloved finger, and if he wanted, he could pretend she was just sleeping.

He slid the photo across the table. "Who is she?"

Doreen blinked and looked away. Her foot jiggled, bouncing up and down beneath the table, squishing in her vomit.

"She was murdered last week. And she was found with your counterfeit hundreds shoved in her mouth."

Doreen froze. Her eyes went wide, wild, and she flicked a single panicked glance his way. She snarled and looked away a moment later, wiping at a line of tears that had slipped from the corner of one eye.

"Why did she have the money you counterfeited, Doreen?"

She shook her head, closing her eyes. Her foot jiggled faster, sending warm vomit across the cold floor.

"Did you guys have anything to do with her death?" Doreen and Aaron and Aaron's goon had been locked up at the time of the girl's killing, but maybe something else had happened.

Doreen's hands slammed down on the table. Her wrists strained in her cuffs, and her face twisted, fury and disgust tearing her apart. And something else. Guilt, a cresting wave of guilt in the depths of her eyes swallowing her whole. "I'd never hurt any of them! This shouldn't have happened!"

"Who was she?" Ethan pushed the picture closer, right between Doreen's hands. "And who are they? Who are you talking about?"

Doreen's face fell. Her head hung between her shoulders. She breathed in, a ragged inhale, and her thin shoulders shook inside her prison jumpsuit. Slowly, she leaned back, hands sliding on the tabletop until she was slouching in her seat. Vomit had dried to her jumpsuit, flaking off in chunks.

She bit her lip. Shook her head. "I'm sorry," she whispered, "but I can't. I can't turn against Mother."

His milk had gone sour and his cupboards were empty. The last of his sandwich bread was gone, and he had only a bottle of ketchup and two beers in his fridge. Grumbling, Ethan grabbed his cell and his keys and headed for his car as he sent a quick text. When he drove out of his complex, two sedans pulled out from a side street to tail him. He glared at his rearview, as if he could transfer that glare to his stalkers.

He knew they were snapping pictures of his car. Of the back of his head.

Fifteen minutes later, he pulled into the grocery store parking lot. More photographers had arrived, parking at the same time he did and hurrying out of their cars, not even bothering to shut their doors as they raced to him, snapping picture after picture and shouting question after question.

"What's going on with you and the president? Are you guys fighting?"

"What are your arguments about?"

"Why are you and the president breaking up?"

"What will you do after you and the president break up?"

Ethan kept his head down and shouldered his way through the crowd until he got to the sliding doors of the grocery.

The manager stood outside, his arms crossed, glowering at the photographers. He gave Ethan a quick nod. Ethan skirted him, ducking into the store.

"You know the rules!" the manager shouted at the restless photographers left behind. "Not a one of you is allowed in my store. If I see a hint of any one of you pricks, I'll call the cops. Got it?" He waited, glaring, as the photographers grumbled back at him.

Ethan grabbed a basket and moved fast, picking up milk and bread and eggs, sandwich meat and apples. A few vegetables. Another case of beer.

Done, he headed for the registers, ignoring the stares of the other shoppers and the conversations about him that no one even tried to hide.

"That's *him*. That's the guy who turned the president gay."

"Such a shame. I really liked President Spiers before. I can't believe he'd throw everything away for a *man*."

His teeth ground together and his fingers flexed on the handles of his basket.

Finally, it was his turn to check out. He waited as the bored college girl scanned his items, staring at him while she mechanically moved through the motions of bagging.

His eyes caught on a glossy magazine behind her head. One of the trashy ones, weekly celebrity gossip and outright lies.

Across the front cover, a picture of him at the airport in DC from just this past Sunday. Grumpy, anguished over leaving Jack, and fed up with the press, he'd pushed through the photographers with a dark scowl on his face. Someone had gotten a picture of that moment, and it was all there, on every checkout aisle, every newsstand. Him, looking furious and wounded and struggling to keep it all together.

Shout lines screamed over the bottom of the photo, across the cover of the magazine. *"It's Over!"* *"Relationship on the Rocks."* *"Keeping up appearances, but for how long?"* *"Sources inside the White House talk screaming matches and separate bedrooms."*

"Thirty-six seventeen." The college girl stared at him, chewing her gum.

He slid his card, his cheeks burning, and refused to look up. Refused to look at the magazine again. He gritted his teeth and tapped his feet, impatience burning through him.

The college girl moved slowly, as if she couldn't be more bored. She smacked her gum as she passed him his receipt. He snatched it, hefted his bags in one hand and his beer in the other, and turned away.

"Jeez. Guess I'd be grumpy too if I was getting dumped." Her voice was soft but snide, spoken under her breath.

He froze. Closed his eyes. *Just walk away.* He could feel the eyes of the entire store staring at him, their eyeballs peeling back his skin, flaying him open until he felt exposed. Raw.

He started walking again, heading for the door where the manager still waited, glaring at the photographers and him in turn.

Damn it, it wasn't even true. Why did the headlines get to him? Why did he feel gut-punched every time he read about something horrible happening to him and Jack on the glossy spreads?

Because what if one day—soon—it becomes real? What if this is your future? Beer and bread and an empty apartment, and the media hounding you until you snap? And there's no Jack, nothing to make it all worthwhile?

He should have schooled himself to something neutral, something better than his ferocious scowl. Hell, even Shepherd had told him to start looking better in front of the media, and if there was one person who didn't care at all about him, it was Shepherd. But he couldn't, he just couldn't. Couldn't pretend that the media spotlight wasn't wearing on him, grinding him down. The rawness of leaving Jack over and over, and the forever that seemed to stretch until they saw each other again, mixed with the ravaging frustration of having to deal with his stalkers day in and day out.

He didn't know what he looked like walking out of the store, but the tight clench of his jaw, the way he blinked fast, trying to stop the heat building behind his eyes, and the clamp of his lips, didn't bode well.

Cameras flashed, photographers hounding him to his car. He dumped his groceries in the backseat and shouldered through the mob to slide behind the wheel. Questions peppered him from everywhere, almost as fast as the strobing camera flashes. Around the parking lot, the world had come to a standstill, moms in minivans frozen while loading their trunks, little old men standing and staring in front of their shopping carts. Teens on skateboards, watching with their hands covering snickering smiles.

He revved his engine three times, as much warning as he could give, before accelerating out of the parking lot. Even still, he nearly ran over a photographer jumping in for a last daring picture.

The drive back to his apartment was deathly silent. He didn't turn on the radio. Didn't do anything except listen to the smack of his tires against the slushy streets, the hum and whine as he turned and braked and finally came to a stop in his complex.

Sighing, he leaned back, gripping the steering wheel until his arms shook.

When would it end? How long could this go on?

Was he asking about the media… or about him and Jack?

He'd endure just about anything to keep what he'd found with Jack. Keep their relationship strong and vibrant. Keep what they'd discovered together—were still discovering together. A love that had redefined his whole world. His whole life.

For that? He'd endure it all.

Would Jack?

Swallowing, he hauled himself out of the car and grabbed his groceries, heading upstairs to his apartment, trying to blank out his mind.

8

Air Force One

Jack stared at nothing in the conference room aboard Air Force One, idly spinning back and forth in his office chair. The room was empty, his papers spread clear across the table, and President Puchkov's proposal lay open in front of him.

He heaved a heavy sigh. Only a few more hours and then he'd be with President Puchkov again, trying to navigate his way through the Russian president's tricks and games. He still didn't know what to make of their time in Prague. Puchkov had pushed hard, but had given Jack the world's second-most-wanted man in exchange. And then, everything after, from being called a Russian faggot to Puchkov slipping him a folder with a potentially world-altering alliance offer.

If only Ethan were there with him. Ethan would distract him. Make him laugh. Hold his hand. Talk through their options again with Jack, for the seven thousandth time.

Which way was right? What was correct? Engage with Puchkov? To what end? What were Puchkov's motivations for reaching out to Jack? Would this help or hurt? Save lives, or lead to more pain? More suffering? Could the US and Russia *actually* work together? They'd done so once, almost ninety years ago, and changed the course of history. Stopped a war and the spread of terror across Europe.

Could the same thing be done again? Halt the horrors of the Caliphate from spreading around the globe?

Leading the world to war was bone-shakingly terrifying. His mind spun, endless scenarios and endless possibilities crowding for attention. Lives saved versus lives lost. Benefit versus cost. He didn't want to be so cold, so matter-of-fact that he made his decisions based on charts and percentages.

He wanted to make a difference. Make things better.

His cell phone, buried under loose sheets from General Bradford's most recent analysis, buzzed, clattering on the table.

It was as if Ethan could read his mind, even so far away.

[I believe in you.]

His smile unfolded slowly, until his cheeks hurt. *I needed that.*

[You alright?]

He blew air out his lips, buzzing them as he slumped. *I'm nervous.* Not second-guessing. He wasn't the type for second-guessing. But sitting alone, fretting over how his choices would play out? Yeah. That was all him.

[You are, without a doubt, the best man to be doing this, Jack.]

His heart seemed to swell, filling with all the love he had for Ethan—every smile, every daydream, every moment they had together. He was warm all over, from his fingers to his toes, awed by the confidence Ethan put in him. How had he earned that? He didn't know, and he probably never would.

But Ethan's confidence helped shore up the crumbling edges of his own, beaten down by endless nights circling around and around the weight of his decision. Taking direct military action, righting a world that had gone sideways and let darkness and terror grow too large. The Caliphate had attacked Europe, attacked Asia, Africa, and the Middle East.

Had sown devastation around the world. Shattered lives.

There would be losses from combating the Caliphate, though. More folded flags and more marble headstones erected in Arlington.

He knew exactly what it felt like when your soldier didn't come home. When all you had left was a folded flag.

And there he was, circling around his choices, over and over again.

Enough. Jack closed his eyes, breathing deep. He let Ethan's words fill him, let his love and his conviction slide into his soul. If he couldn't stand under the weight of his choices alone, then he'd stand with Ethan. On the bedrock of Ethan's belief in him.

You are my rock. I don't know if I could do this without you.

[I'm here.]
I'm so glad you are.

He shifted, trying to stop the downward spiral of his thoughts. Anytime his mind veered at all toward wondering how he'd manage without Ethan, thoughts of a dusty side street in Ethiopia roared to the front of his mind, and bullets cracked in his dreams, and then he was screaming, reaching for Ethan as Ethan lay in a pool of his spreading blood, his eyes cold and lifeless.

What are you up to?

[Still at the office. Everyone left early to grab a beer. I'm reviewing case notes.]

It had been stupid, but when Ethan told Jack about the murdered girl who had crashed into his counterfeit investigation, Jack's palms had slicked with sweat and his heart had thundered in his chest for the rest of the night. Ethan had been charged with diving in front of a bullet for Jack, had held his own when the world fell apart, and had saved him—and the world—when everything was on the line. But, still, the thought of a murderer so close to Ethan, of Ethan investigating financial crimes while skirting a murder investigation, sat unsteady in his heart.

No happy hour for you?

[Bad idea. Would turn into a media circus. And I wasn't invited.]
I'm sorry.

[Don't be. Rather be texting you anyway. :)]

And just like that, he was smiling again.

Until Agent Collard poked his head into the conference room. "We're coming up on LaGuardia, Mr. President. We land in twenty minutes."

He thanked Collard with a small smile and spun back to the table. Glared at his papers spread everywhere. Closed his eyes and let his head fall back when his gaze wandered to Puchkov's proposal.

We're landing in a few. I have to clean up.

When Ethan had been on the detail, he'd always wander in and help Jack clean the tornado that he created whenever he had a chance to spread out. Laughing at him, Ethan would play along, sliding papers into folders and then stacking them in Jack's mercurial filing system: stuff to do soon, stuff to put off, stuff to be read on the toilet, and stuff that could be forgotten. He'd made up new categories on the fly for Ethan to laugh at. Something they'd shared, both before and after they were together.

After they'd gotten together, Ethan would sneak in kisses when they were done clearing the table. And once, Jack had sat on the conference table's edge, drawing him close until Ethan had laid him back, kissing his neck, and then they'd nearly rolled right off when they'd gotten carried away kissing and missed the landing announcement.

Luckily, Collard had been at the door. Jack hadn't known at the time, but Collard had reamed Ethan behind the privacy screen in the Beast, while Jack and Secretary Wall had traded notes in the backseat.

[Any new files? :)]

There was, but Jack wouldn't admit it. Stuff to read after nightmares.

Sadly, it's all stuff I have to do. One big file.

He tucked everything back into his briefcase and sat back down, letting the thrum of the plane rise into his bones.

[I'll be online all night. Call whenever. I'll be here.]

They'd miss their scheduled Skype call, but Jack refused to let a day pass without seeing Ethan's face and hearing his voice. *I'll call as soon as I can.*

[I believe in you. I love you.]

You are my rock. I love you too.

From LaGuardia, Jack was driven to the UN, running a full motorcade with lights and sirens and the NYPD closing off streets and guiding him through the traffic. Agents Collard and Daniels had their serious faces on, stone masks behind mirrored shades and thin lips. Jack sat in the back of the SUV, watching New York City roll by outside the black-tinted windows. His fingers tapped on his thighs, an endless thrum.

They parked in the underground garage beneath the UN Conference Building, an army of Secret Service agents surrounding Jack the moment he stepped out of the SUV. Daniels grabbed Jack's briefcase and passed it to Welby, out of the close detail and following behind the main delegation. Lawrence Irwin and Secretary of State Elizabeth Wall stepped out of their own SUVs and joined Jack at the elevators. Behind them, Secret Service agents and his staff hung back, almost oppressively silent.

Jack wanted to scream.

The ride up to the fourth floor, the top floor, seemed to take an eternity. Collard and Daniels stood in front of him in the elevator, hands clasped before them, legs spread wide, like they were Roman Legionnaires facing off against the world. In a way, they were.

They cleared the hallway off the elevator before Jack stepped out and then moved in close, staying just behind his shoulders as Jack headed for the Ambassador's Terrace, the rooftop patio and bar for ambassadors, heads of state, and world leaders.

For now, it was host to the Security Council of the United Nations, the five permanent member nations—the United States, Russia, the United Kingdom, France, and China—and the ten nonpermanent member nations currently in rotation, along with their heads of state, their staff, and ambassadors.

It was a smorgasbord of political power. A who's who of countries, policy makers, and influencers.

Some of them supported Jack and his relationship with Ethan.

Others vehemently opposed him. Had railed against him in their countries. Had withheld their hands from him when he went in for a handshake, or turned away entirely, as if he wasn't even there. Or worse. As if he was something disgusting.

Heads turned, everyone staring as Jack strode onto the terrace surrounded by his detail. Eyes slid over him, their slick, hot slide shivering down his spine.

God, he wished Ethan were there. He'd wanted him, desperately, at the G20 over Thanksgiving, but it would have been impossible to bring him along. Not with their commitment to keeping themselves low-key and Ethan wanting to rebuild his career in the Secret Service. If he had asked, though, would Ethan have accepted? He didn't want to know. Didn't want to face it if Ethan had turned him down. Or worse, if Ethan had said yes because he thought he had to.

But, what would it feel like, having Ethan at his side, his acknowledged partner, during these events? It would feel better than winning the presidency; he was sure of it.

All the other spouses were there. Why not Ethan, too?

He shoved that down. Tried to focus on the terrace and the reactions to his entrance.

There were some smiles. Some waves. The British prime minister sent him a terse smile. South Africa's president nodded. Germany's chancellor gave a stately tip of the head. Canada waved and sent a big smile, but that was Canada's reaction to nearly everyone.

Most everyone stared. Japan's delegation. China's delegation. Cameroon's. France's president and his staff.

And then there were those who despised him.

The Gambia's president snorted and turned his back. Nigeria's president started shouting at his delegation, pointing at Jack and laughing boisterously. It wasn't a friendly kind of laugh. It was the kind of laugh a bully would make.

Pakistan's president led his delegation off the terrace.

Jack straightened his jacket, clearing his throat. He didn't regret the choices he'd made. He would never regret Ethan. Never regret their love.

But that didn't make the consequences any easier.

"Mr. President!"

And there was President Sergey Puchkov, striding across the terrace, his long legs outpacing the hulking Presidential Security Services agents behind him. Puchkov waved and called out to Jack again. "Mr. President, it is good to see you again." He held out his hand.

Jack took it with a smile. "Mr. President. You shocked the hell out of me at the G20. Are you usually so dramatic?"

Puchkov laughed, loud and full. His head bobbed back and forth, one hand waving in the air. "Mmm, occasionally. I can be known to have some fun." He winked. "Come! Join me, Mr. President. Let us have a drink together."

"We've got a great deal to discuss, President Puchkov."

"In a while, Mr. President." Puchkov beckoned across the terrace again, toward the crowd of heads of state, ambassadors, and delegates. "Come. Let us drink first. Get to know one another. Before we try to build an alliance and change this world."

Jack swallowed but pasted a bright grin on his face. "I assume you're drinking vodka?"

Puchkov laughed, and they fell into step together, slow strides through the crowd. Agents from Jack's Secret Service and Puchkov's Security Services jogged ahead, staging around an empty table and a couple of cushioned rattan couches beside a heater. "Mr. President," Puchkov scoffed. "While I am sure your New York City offers only the best vodka, nothing can beat Siberian vodka strained through diesel engine."

"I'm not sure I could be that brave."

"Takes a year away from your life with every shot." Puchkov winked and waved over a waiter balancing glasses of champagne. "I will have a whiskey," Puchkov ordered and then turned to Jack, his eyebrows raised.

He needed to keep his wits around Puchkov. "Vodka tonic, please."

Puchkov scoffed as the waiter vanished, an agent each from the Secret Service and Puchkov's security shadowing him back to the bar. "You dilute your vodka?" He pretended to glare at Jack, seeming to assess his worth based on his drink order alone.

"How was your flight?" Jack's molars scraped over each other. When he spoke with world leaders, there was always an agenda. A set dialogue, questions to ask and statements to give. Small talk wasn't on the menu, except at NATO, where the delegation thrived on cloakroom gossip and bar-side chats. How was he supposed to make small talk with the Russian president?

"Was good, was good." Puchkov relaxed, unbuttoning his jacket and leaning back with a sigh. "Is always easy, coming to the United States." He paused. "And yours, Mr. President?"

"Fine. Short." Jack grinned. "DC isn't far."

"Yes. Playing host to the United Nations. Perhaps, one day, Russia will host the headquarters."

A subtle dig at the United States' standing in the world, her superpower status Russia always sought to knock down.

The waiter reappeared, saving Jack by passing over Puchkov's whiskey and Jack's vodka tonic. Puchkov held his glass up for a toast, and then they drank. The agents who had stalked the waiter and the bartender took up their posts behind their respective leaders, fierce masks of stone firmly in place.

"Do you have any family, Mr. President?" Jack tried to change the direction of their repartee. He kicked himself a moment later. Of course Puchkov had family. He hadn't popped out of the Siberian wilderness, harvested from the permafrost and raised by wolves.

"I have a Russian pair. Two ex-wives." Puchkov smiled. One hand moved while he talked, big gestures in the air. "That was long ago. Now, I am devoted civil servant. I serve my people." He took another sip, his eyes pinching at the corners. "And you, Mr. President? Mr. Reichenbach is not here with you tonight?"

Jack shook his head. He didn't trust himself to speak. He drank instead, sipping the vodka tonic and squinting over the East River. Snow huddled on both banks and clung to New York's skeleton trees.

"He is working in your state of Iowa, yes?" Puchkov peered at Jack, practically staring.

So the Russian intelligence system was keeping tabs on them. Jack smiled, big and bold, and turned back to Puchkov. "That's right. In Iowa. Catching bad guys in the Midwest."

Puchkov laughed. "Like a cowboy. Chasing down the bad guys on a horse, yes? Does he have a hat? One of those big ones?"

Was Puchkov making fun of them? Sometimes he couldn't tell. Jack tried to picture it, though. Ethan as a cowboy in the Old West. He chuckled. "No hat. No horse."

Silence fell over the pair as they both drank again. Jack's thumb stroked down the edge of his class, tapping where Puchkov couldn't see.

"It... must be difficult," Puchkov finally said, speaking softly. His lips were pursed, and he stared into his glass of whiskey. "To be separated by such distance. Like Moscow to Prague. Very far." His eyes flicked up, meeting Jack's.

Jack's throat clenched. The vodka he drank soured in his stomach, sitting heavy like lead. His lips thinned, and all he could do was nod, holding Puchkov's gaze. Behind him, he could just hear Agent Collard, his voice a whisper of breath. "Asshole."

Puchkov's gaze jumped, moving like a snake to something beyond Jack. Heavy, boisterous laughter erupted, and then footsteps, and from the throng of world leaders on the terrace, the Nigerian president emerged, heading for their table.

Puchkov jerked his chin toward their approaching visitor. "This man, he was disrespectful to you at the G20, yes?"

Jack's eyes narrowed. His heart hammered and his blood roared through him as he watched the Nigerian president come closer. "Yeah."

At the handshake line, the official reception for the G20, the Nigerian president had stepped away from Jack, sniffing and scoffing and turning away with both hands held dramatically up in the air. "I don't shake hands with your kind," he'd growled in his deep voice. "We do not allow or encourage abominations in my country."

The world's media had caught it all. The clip played over and over in between football games on Thanksgiving Day, on political commentary shows over the weekend, and still kept turning up, hauled out for dissection whenever any of Jack's increasingly hostile Republican colleagues wanted to sling mud.

It wasn't the first moment Jack had been washed in humiliation, had bathed in furious mortification, and it wouldn't be the last. He'd known it would happen. Had tried to prepare for it.

But how could you prepare for *that*? He'd wanted to scream. Wanted to storm away. Wanted to call Ethan and hear his voice, take the next flight back to the US, to Iowa, and grab Ethan and run. Run away from the world's spotlight, from everyone's censure and criticism.

Instead, he'd smiled politely, nodded, and moved down the line to the president of The Gambia, who'd pretended Jack didn't exist. Saudi Arabia's king came next, and he had embraced Jack, kissing him on both cheeks, his weathered hands like old leather on Jack's skin.

Puchkov leaned back, steepling his fingers as his elbows rested on the chair's woven arms. He watched the Nigerian president amble toward them and settle into a chair beside Puchkov.

"Mr. President!" the Nigerian president crowed, clapping Puchkov on the shoulder. "How wonderful to see you again!"

Puchkov said nothing. His lips quirked up on one side.

Jack sat silent, ignored. His blood boiled, but he stayed still.

"Mr. President." The Nigerian president leaned back, his long black overcoat spreading around his portly body, his fedora tipped back on his bald head. "Do you have a moment to discuss our nuclear partnership? We would like to accelerate the construction of the two nuclear plants you promised to our country. Thanks to our oil exports, Nigeria's economy is booming." He laughed, a thick gold chain at his neck flashing.

Puchkov's head tilted, just so. His lips pursed, and his index fingers rested against them for a moment. "That project has been canceled."

The Nigerian president froze. Stopped breathing.

"The Russian Federation is cancelling all future work projects in Nigeria, in fact."

"What?" Breathless, the Nigerian president stared. "Mr. President," he chuckled, reaching for Puchkov. "What has brought this on? Our countries have grown close—"

"*You*, Mr. President, have brought this on yourself." Puchkov held up two fingers, almost in the Nigerian president's face. His voice was soft, almost like he was talking to a young child. "This is twice now you have paid great disrespect to my friend, my ally." He gestured to Jack. "You think you can disrespect Russia's friends and suffer no consequences? No, Russia is a better ally than that."

It was Jack's turn to stop breathing.

The Nigerian president sputtered. He turned to Jack, his eyes narrowed. "Mr. President," he tried, leaning forward toward Jack. "You have to understand. The choices you've made. We simply cannot support this lifestyle—"

Puchkov stood, grasping his whiskey in one hand. "President Spiers, I believe we have business to attend to, yes? I will join you to speak about these things now."

Jack rose silently.

"President Puchkov!" The Nigerian president reached out again, grasping Puchkov's sleeve. "You can't do this!"

"Mr. President." Puchkov smoothed his jacket, pulling free. "Russia's economy has also grown. Especially our oil sector. Russia no longer has any need of your oil exports. We will cease all business with your country. Immediately." Puchkov gestured for Jack to lead the way, back across the terrace and into the UN.

"You will regret this!" Storming up, the Nigerian president stomped his foot, almost spitting in his fury. "I will vote *no* on your resolution!"

"We do not need your vote." And with that, Puchkov buttoned his suit and followed Jack through the crowds.

Jack traded long looks with Agents Collard and Daniels as they stepped off the terrace and waited for Puchkov. The Russian president appeared a moment after, warmly shaking hands with the Belarus ambassador before striding to Jack. He clasped his hands together and grinned. "Shall we change the world, Mr. President?"

They ended up in the empty chambers of the Security Council, spreading out on the semicircular delegates' table. Jack took his briefcase back from Welby and pulled out his papers and his reading glasses. For hours, he and Puchkov walked through each scenario, through what they were willing to provide to the alliance and the roles their militaries would jointly play in an invasion force. Sharing bases. Sharing forces. Command authority. Splitting costs.

When the words began to blur together, they took a break, stretching and grabbing cups of coffee long gone cold.

Jack had to ask. "Your economy has lost half a percent in its GDP. Our intelligence says your oil exploration in the north and the Arctic hasn't gone as well as you hoped."

Puchkov smiled, sly, and the lines in his face furrowed, exhaustion warring with his humor. "We still don't need *their* oil."

Jack stayed silent for a moment, but returned Puchkov's smile. "Thank you."

Puchkov waved him away. "Is nothing, Mr. President." He stood, rolling his shoulders. "We should discuss the language in our proposed resolution—"

Jack glanced at the clock mounted above the phoenix painting stretching on the far wall, behind Puchkov. "Do you mind if we take a short break? I… need to make a phone call."

Puchkov's eyebrows shot up. "Something to talk with your advisors about? We can discuss, Mr. President. Is there something we must adjust?"

"No. It's personal. I call Ethan every night. One way we stay close." He pointed to the clock. "It's already late."

Puchkov tapped a pen against his palm. "I need to stretch my legs. I think I will take a walk. I will return shortly." He winked, tossed his pen on the papers, and headed out, his hands in his pockets.

Jack slumped in the Pakistani delegation's main chair at the Security Council table and spun his laptop toward him. A few quick strokes, and he had the secured signal the White House IT guys had put on his laptop enabled. A few more, and then he was opening Skype and dialing Ethan's number.

The call answered, the screen onlining to reveal Ethan hovering in front of his computer as if he'd just run across his apartment to answer. He was shirtless and his hair was damp.

"Hey!" Ethan beamed. "Lemme grab a shirt." He disappeared.

"You don't have to!" Jack's jaw had fallen open and his mouth had gone dry, his tongue hot and heavy and useless when Ethan had appeared, his bare chest in front of the camera. He swallowed. "I mean, you can. If—if you want to. But... you don't have to." He shrugged, a helpless smile tugging on his lips.

Ethan reappeared, his head poking back on camera. Wide eyes, and a shy grin, and... shirtless. He sat back down, his cheeks flushed, but cleared his throat. "How is it going?"

"Good so far. President Puchkov and I are making progress."

"You guys done for the night?"

"Nope. Still working hard. He stepped out." Jack spun his laptop, showing Ethan the silent Security Council chambers. "And that—" He pointed inside the camera's feed to the spread of papers and files strewn across the council's table. "Is our big mess."

Ethan laughed as Jack spun the laptop back around. Jack folded his arms, braced them against the tabletop, and leaned close to the screen, smiling. His eyes, though, kept bouncing down to Ethan's bare chest. His tanned skin. His muscles. His chest hair. "How was your day?" He forced his gaze back up.

"Good." He talked about his case, and in the middle of walking through a piece of evidence they were puzzling over, he crossed his arms. His biceps joined the call.

Jack groaned, his head falling forward. Ethan laughed out loud. "Jack... *Really?*"

When Jack looked up, he saw the nervousness Ethan was trying to hide in his eyes. The corner of his lip being bitten. Jack sighed. "You caught me." He grinned. "I'm sorry. I am so attracted to you."

And there was the full flush, staining Ethan's cheeks and chest crimson as he looked down. "I'm... uh... *really* attracted to you, too."

It was sweet, the way they were flirting. Like they didn't devour each other every weekend they could. Like it was still new and fragile.

In some ways, it was.

A creaking door across the chamber made Jack look up. President Puchkov came striding back in, holding two paper cups of coffee. He held one out for Jack.

"President Puchkov is back." Jack smiled at Ethan on-screen. "Gotta get back to work."

Ethan nodded. He blew a silent kiss to the camera.

"I love you, Ethan."

Ethan's eyes went wide.

Jack laughed. Of course Ethan wouldn't have expected him to say it out loud in front of another head of state. But he would. He'd say it in front of everyone. In front of the whole world.. Endlessly.

"I love you too," Ethan said softly. His eyes were blazing, burning up with love for Jack, a heat he could feel even a thousand miles away.

Jack blew a kiss as Ethan waved. The screen cut out. He closed his laptop, taking a deep breath, and then looked up, meeting Puchkov's gaze.

Puchkov smiled. He headed back for their messy papers, setting down Jack's coffee for him before he tugged one of their chicken-scratch drafts free. "So, Jack—" He stopped. Turned to Jack when he drew near. "May I call you Jack?"

Jack sipped his coffee and nodded. "Please do."

"And you will call me Sergey." Puchkov dipped his head and turned back to the draft. "So, Jack, I think we must adjust this sentence here. We must make it clear we are partners in this section as well as the others…"

9

Des Moines

Ringing speared through Ethan's sleep.

He jerked back, rising from a facedown slump in his pillow to his elbows and fumbled for his cell on the bed.

It was Jack.

He swiped to answer, flopping to his back and scrubbing his hand over his face. "Hey, baby."

Jack exhaled, breathless relief crackling over the line. "*Hey.*"

Ethan blinked hard and scooted up on his bed. "You all right?"

"*Getting there.*" He sounded shaky. "*Hearing your voice is helping.*"

"Nightmare?"

Jack sighed. "*Yeah.*" He swallowed. "*I'm sorry I woke you up. It's early. You should go back to sleep—*"

"Hey, it's fine." Ethan moved the phone away from his mouth so Jack wouldn't hear him yawn. "I'm glad you called. I don't care what time it is."

"*Thanks.*" Jack's voice was soft, almost a whisper.

"What happened?"

A long sigh, and Ethan heard Jack moving in his hotel bed, blankets and pillows shuffling around him. "*Al-Karim. When he had you. Made that video. But this time—*"

Jack didn't need to say it. Didn't need to fill in the blanks. It had been only blind luck that he hadn't had his throat slit in the first video. If Jeff Gottschalk had had his way, Ethan would have been killed then, on-screen, and Jack would have watched his beheaded body hit the dust as he stood next to the man who had made Ethan's capture possible. Who had offered Jack false words of comfort and friendship.

"I'm here." Ethan's heart ached. What he would give to be there, holding Jack. "I'm here. I'm all right."

Distraction, that's what Jack needed. Something that wasn't about war or terror, about darkness and nightmares. Something that would make Jack laugh. "I have a confession to make."

"*Huh?*"

"Do you remember that big speech you'd recycle on the campaign trail? About American strength and prosperity?"

"*Yeah...*" Jack sounded confused.

Ethan grinned. "So, Scott and I were off duty one night. We rotated out, and Daniels and Inada were taking the lead. It was... Boulder. No. Salt Lake City. It all blurs together. We stayed in the hotel and watched your speech on TV and... we made a drinking game out of how many times you said 'American strength and American prosperity'."

Jack burst out laughing, music to Ethan's ears. "*How drunk did you get?*"

"Pretty wasted. Scott gave up first. We were knocking back tequila we got from the gas station half a block down from the hotel. It wasn't pretty."

"*I guess I did use that phrase a lot.*"

"A lot? It was on bumper stickers, buttons, billboards, posters. Hats. T-shirts." Ethan kept listing everything that had Jack's pseudo-slogan. "It was everywhere."

"*It was a good call to action. American strength and American prosperity are things to be proud of.*"

"Okay, I know that was a line from the speech. Do I need to get my tequila?"

Jack laughed again. "*At four thirty in the morning? No!*" He kept laughing, but then quieted, and Ethan listened to his soft breathing over the line. Then, Jack spoke. "*Do you remember the first day we met?*"

"Monday, July eleventh." He didn't even have to think.

"*Wow.*" Jack's voice was full of wonder, a smile building in between the letters.

"Secret Service provides protection for major candidates one hundred and twenty days before the election. That was the day I reported to you."

Snorting, Jack chuckled. *"That was almost sweet."*

"You were wearing your blue suit. The one that makes your eyes look like stars. And a yellow tie. Everyone was teasing you about the tie. I thought you looked amazing. Presidential."

Silence. *"That made up for it,"* he breathed. *"You thought I looked amazing? Even then?"*

"Always, Jack. I've always thought you were amazing. And looked amazing."

"You intimidated the hell out of me."

"What?" Ethan frowned. "I didn't mean—"

"You were the first real thing that meant I could actually win. I was on the way to the White House. The poll numbers were there, but it wasn't until you walked in the door that I realized I actually—seriously—had a chance at winning. At being the president."

"And I intimidated you?"

"You can be fierce, Ethan." Jack was smiling. Ethan could hear it in his voice. *"You were... larger than life. The head of my Secret Service detail on the campaign. My new shadow. And I didn't see you really smile. Not once."* He paused. *"Until Christmas."*

"I thought you were going to report me after Christmas."

"Why would I do that? You were looking out for your team. For your guys. I thought it was great. Made me realize there was more to you. You were someone I wanted to get to know."

Ethan snorted. "It's admirable, you know, how you achieve the goals you set for yourself."

Jack laughed again, and Ethan grinned as he chewed on his lip. He grabbed a pillow and held it close, as if it were Jack.

"There are some days," Jack began, sighing, *"that I wish I'd never run for president. But being president brought me to you, and I wouldn't trade us for anything."*

His throat clenched, his heart thundering. "Neither would I. Not for anything."

"*Even with—*"

"Not for anything." Lying in the dark in an empty apartment while Jack was shaking off a nightmare wasn't ideal, but it was *something*. It was *theirs*, a future they'd worked hard for, built despite all odds stacked against them.

"*Thank you,*" Jack whispered. "*I think I needed to hear that.*"

Ethan frowned. "Second thoughts?" He shifted, his feet rubbing together, and rolled onto his side, trying not to let his heart gallop out of control.

"*Fears.*"

He waited. "What about?"

"*If you think the cost is too high for you. If you ever regret—*"

"Never." He sat up, leaning forward, even though Jack couldn't see him and wasn't there. "Never. I would make the same decisions again. Choose this every time." In the silence that followed, Ethan's chest ached, and he pressed his lips together as his palms slicked with sweat. "Would you?"

Jack didn't hesitate. "*Yes.*"

Fears they couldn't name, couldn't face in the daylight, now spoken in whispers over the phone, half a continent between them. Answers Ethan needed to hear more than he could admit. Warmth flooded through him, and a wide smile stretched his cheeks. Made them ache.

"*You still there?*" Sounds over the line, like blankets shuffling. Jack had rolled over.

"Yeah." Ethan cleared his throat. "Yeah, I'm here."

"*It's almost five. I'm going to get up. Head down to the hotel gym. This amazing guy once told me that the best stress relief for a president is working out.*"

"Amazing guy, huh?" He plucked at his sheets, still grinning.

"*He's such a hunk.*"

Chuckling, Ethan fell back in his bed. "Have a good morning, okay?"

"Will you be able to get back to sleep?"

"Yeah. I'll be fine." He chewed on his upper lip. "I'm really glad you called."

"Me too. Thank you." Jack chuckled. *" 'Baby'."*

Ethan laughed at his cute greeting that had slipped out in his sleepy state. He'd never called Jack "baby", or any other pet names. It seemed strange, somehow, to call the president of the United States "baby". Maybe there was something else, though. Some other sweet nickname he could give Jack.

"Anytime."

Silence, until Jack spoke again. *"Love you."*

"Love you too."

Jack's address to the UN Security Council was big news. Big enough to break into the daily news cycle on a Friday and keep cameras locked on the deliberations. Ethan had the entire thing streaming live on his cell phone, his headphones plugged in as he worked in his cubicle, waiting for Jack's big moment.

The true deliberations happened behind closed doors, in the consultation rooms off the Security Council chambers. Those conversations would come later, Friday evening and into the night, and even through the weekend, as the delegates debated after Jack delivered his and President Puchkov's joint resolution to the Security Council asking for immediate approval on a joint invasion to combat the Caliphate-held lands in the Middle East.

When the blaring "Breaking News" alert flashed, he rose and headed for the breakroom, pocketing his phone only when he was in sight of the large flat-screen hanging on the wall and tuned in to TNN.

On-screen, Jack was adjusting the microphone. Flipping through his papers, until he had the start of his speech ready to go.

Ethan gripped the edge of a metal folding chair, the legs squeaking as it slid on the linoleum.

"*Good morning,*" Jack began, nodding around the Security Council chambers. "*It has been twenty years since the United States was last here, making a request to the world for global unification in the fight against terrorism. As a nation, and together with the world, we learned a great deal. And we sacrificed too much. I,*" he said, exhaling. His breath shook, just faintly. "*Am a product of choices made twenty years ago.*"

Ethan nodded at the screen, as if he could encourage Jack through the television.

"*We are faced now with a new threat, one that has struck terror into all corners of our globe. The Caliphate has risen in the Middle East, born of the ashes of hate and an ideology that perverts the religion it purports to uphold. Radical sociopaths operate under the veil of Islam, devastating the lives of millions of many faithful, loving Muslims. Hundreds of thousands of people around the world have felt the touch of terror in their lives and have lived through horrors that should never have been.*"

Behind Ethan, footsteps shuffled. Someone entering the breakroom. He didn't turn.

"*For too long, the world has stood without unity. We have not come together against this threat, and the Caliphate has taken advantage of our separations and distance. From strikes in Europe to attacks against their own people, the Caliphate has been left alone, given too much freedom to destroy and devastate. As nations, we have all carried out actions individually—*" He gestured to himself and to President Puchkov, next to him. "*—air strikes and special forces—*"

To the United Kingdom's delegation. "*Air strikes and sophisticated intelligence networking—*"

To the Saudi Arabian delegation. "*Intelligence support, arms and financial backing to those who opposed the Caliphate—*"

He glanced down at his notes briefly. "*And, we have all done what we could to try to welcome those who have escaped from the horrors the Caliphate perpetrates against their own people.*

Accepted refugees who left everything, desperate for a chance at life without fear.

"The Caliphate has taken advantage of our goodwill, though. There has never been a more heartbreaking choice between welcoming people desperate for a chance at living free from the horrors of their devastated homeland hijacked by the forces of terror, and the fear that hidden within these people who need our care is a Trojan horse, waiting to destroy us from within the arms of our compassion. Europe has felt this terror too many times."

Ethan's lips moved with Jack's, reciting the words of the speech. They'd practiced over and over, endlessly tweaking and refining the words and Jack's delivery through the week, until Jack could say it all, his chin held high and without his voice wavering. For Jack, there were too many memories embedded in the speech, too many ghosts hanging in the words and between vowels and consonants.

"I come here today, united at last with a great ally." Jack clapped President Puchkov, sitting next to him, on the shoulder. Puchkov smiled, and he reached back for Jack, gripping his shoulder for a moment before they both let go. Another first for the Security Council. *"Together, we have come to the decision that the continued and ongoing threat posed by the Caliphate must be addressed, and addressed immediately. The Caliphate must be stopped, and their hateful ideology must be eradicated. We offer to the council today a proposed resolution asking for the world to join with us in our fight. Make no mistake. The United States and her ally, the Russian Federation, will take the lead in this effort. And we will act. But, we wish to do so united with the world, and not in opposition to her."*

Jack flipped another page. Subtly rolled his shoulders, a movement so faint Ethan was probably the only one who noticed. But he knew Jack's body, knew it inside out, all his movements and quirks and what they meant. "Bring it home, Jack," he breathed. "Almost done."

"The dangers of inaction are clear. We have already seen and felt the tragedies of the Caliphate's actions. No one, anywhere in the world, has done anything to deserve these attacks, these horrors.

Most especially not the civilians held hostage in the lands captured by the Caliphate. We, in this chamber, have a duty to the world. To address head-on the horrors that can lead to unspeakable tragedy. To set courses in history toward safety and security for all nations and all peoples.

"We ask today that the world join us. Join our will. Join our resolve. Rise to what our joint responsibility to this world is: to secure peace and freedom in every place, and serve the peoples of this great world. New realities have shaped our lives, and it is up to us to react justly to such realities, to choose to support freedom and liberty for all, and to make true peace a lasting reality. Our strength as a people—as a global force—lies in our bonds of unity and our steadfast commitments to supporting one another. Our compassion for our fellow man, and our resolve to stand united against the darkness, and to do battle with those who choose hatred."

Ethan watched Jack press his hands to the table, flattening them. Another of Jack's signs, a quirk that revealed his stress, his need to ground himself. He'd seen it, learned what it meant, and he swallowed hard as he watched.

"We bring before the Security Council our proposed resolution for immediate action against the Caliphate for your review and your vote. Thank you."

Jack leaned back, breathing deeply as he schooled his expression to confidence. Ethan watched the slow rise and fall of his tie over his chest.

Puchkov stood, clapping and reaching for Jack, pumping his hand as he squeezed his shoulder. The delegate from the United Kingdom rose and clapped, as did the Saudi Arabian delegation. The Germans nodded.

France's delegate glowered over their glasses. Japan's stared. The Gambia's president's eyes narrowed. Nigeria's president scowled.

Ethan watched as the camera panned over the Security Council chambers, the anchors talking over the Security Council president announcing a recess for deliberations. He tried to watch Jack through the movements of people, through the hustle and bustle on-screen, but he lost Jack as he stood with Puchkov, greeting the British prime minister and ambassador.

"You were reciting the speech as it happened."

Jumping, Ethan whirled, glaring when he spotted Becker at his side. "Jesus Christ, Becker. Warn a guy."

"I did. I said 'Hey' when I got here."

Ethan hadn't heard a thing. He turned back to the TV, but the camera feed had cut out, turned to talking heads back in the studio dissecting Jack's speech. Words like "defining" and "powerful" were being tossed around. "Monumental." He smiled.

"Wow. That's only the second time I've seen you smile. Ever."

He shrugged. Turned to Becker and tried to tune out the TV. "That speech was a big deal. He worked hard on it. With the speechwriter and on his delivery."

Becker frowned. "How'd you know it all?"

"We practiced together. Until we could both recite it in our sleep."

Becker's frown deepened. He stared at Ethan, questions bouncing in his eyes. His lips thinned, though. As if he was holding back his words, trying not to speak.

"Reichenbach! Becker! My office! Now!"

Jumping, Becker spun, just catching the back of Shepherd as their SSA stormed out of the breakroom and headed back to his office.

"What now?" Ethan sighed, filing out with Becker in tow.

"What did I do?" Becker grumbled behind him.

Shepherd motioned for them to shut his door when they entered. He didn't ask them to sit.

"Why the *hell* is the head of the Midwest FBI office calling me bitching about you two?"

Becker's gaze darted to Ethan.

Ethan rolled his eyes. Always, always with the FBI. "Sir, we were following leads on the heartland counterfeiting ring. The Jane Doe corpse. We interviewed the suspects we have in custody, and the woman keeps mentioning someone. 'Mother,' she calls her. Says she can't go against her. We did a search for any open cases referencing someone with the alias 'Mother.' Ran into some closed FBI files. All we did was request access to the information."

But the FBI acted like they'd gone hog wild through their files, coloring outside their lines and spilling juice boxes and graham cracker crumbs in their toy bin.

"You do know what your job is, right?" Shepherd glared first at Ethan, then Becker. "You do know your job here isn't to be heroes. You're *not* catching a murderer. That's *not* a mystery for you to solve. You're not out to get in the papers. Be famous." He snorted, shaking his head at Ethan. "You are financial crimes. *Financial.* Counterfeiters. Bank fraud. This girl's murderer? That's the FBI's lane. Not yours." His hand came down on his desk. "So stay in your lane! Focus on what you need to get done. Don't get distracted by someone else's job."

Shepherd glared until they both nodded. "Becker, get out of here. Shut the door behind you."

Becker slid out, disappearing like vapor. The door shut softly behind him.

Shepherd hung his head. "Reichenbach, what am I going to do with you? You just won't quit, will you?"

"Sir, we weren't trying to find the murderer. We were just tracking down evidence."

"Be that as it may, you remember what we discussed. Everything you touch is corrupted. Everything you get involved in is open to a hundred different suspicions. You sniffing around in the FBI's case files is a *big* fucking no. They've got something going on with this Mother person. Leave the case to them. Got it?"

Ethan nodded.

"And don't get Becker involved in any of your bullshit. He's a good agent. He's got a good future ahead of him. I want to see him go far." Shepherd sat in his chair, propped his elbows on his desk, and rubbed his hands over his face. "Don't go fucking up this kid's reputation right out of the gate, okay?"

"He *is* a good agent. I like him."

Shepherd glared at him over his fingertips, giving him the hairy eyeball.

"Jesus, Shepherd, I'm not going to destroy the kid."

"Just try to keep him out of the papers, too. I don't need any more scandal in this office."

"What the *hell* are you implying?"

"Just stating facts, Reichenbach. Wherever you go, whoever you're with, you're a target. Think twice about what that means."

His hands clenched, his blood starting to burn within him.

"Will that be all, sir?"

Shepherd nodded. "Keep your head down, Reichenbach."

He strode out, jerking the door open too hard, the glass rattling as the doorknob hit Shepherd's wall. Fuming, he stalked to his cube, glaring at any agent who glanced his way.

In his cube, Becker perched on his chair, staring at the single photo he had of Jack and him. He was holding Jack from behind as they both laughed at Daniels, who had taken the picture in the Rose Garden, tucked out of sight of the public on a weekend. He kept it beneath his monitor, almost hidden from view unless someone was sitting at the keyboard.

Becker's wide eyes found his. "Everything okay?"

"What are you doing in my cube?"

Becker ignored his question. "So what do we do now? Where do we investigate?" Becker slid out of his chair and leaned on the cubicle wall. His gaze wandered back to Ethan's picture.

Ethan turned it over. "We dig into Doreen. She's the link between the money and the girl. And she's smarter than the other jackasses. I'm willing to bet she's the link for the material they got to make those bills."

Becker nodded. He pushed off the wall, heading back to his own cube. Stopped. "You, uh. You guys look happy there." His chin jerked to Ethan's hand, still holding the photo facedown.

A moment, silent. "Thanks," Ethan grunted.

Becker left without another word.

10

Outside the Security Council chambers, Picasso's *Guernica* stretched along one wall, gigantic and grotesque. Harsh lines depicted tragedy and horror: images of death and war and an aerial bombing of civilians from the Spanish Civil War.

Jack, slumped against the wall with his hands in his pockets, stared at the image until his eyes blurred.

Within the consultation rooms behind the chambers, heads of state, ambassadors, and delegates argued, discussions raging back and forth over Jack and Puchkov's proposed resolution.

He'd had to walk away, after hours of talking. Had to take a break.

Footsteps whispering on carpet broke the stillness. He looked up.

President Puchkov ambled for him, one corner of his mouth quirked up. "Calling your Mr. Reichenbach?"

"No. He's still at work. Just…" He waved his hand toward the consultation room. "Getting some air."

Puchkov nodded, lips pursed, and leaned against the wall next to Jack. His head tilted. "This is an ugly picture."

"It's not meant to be pretty."

"Bah."

"I think it's too soft." He felt Puchkov's stare, felt his gaze hit the side of his face. "Picasso wanted to paint the horrors of war. And you're right. It's ugly. Sickening. But—" He sighed. "But war is so much worse than anything anybody could ever paint."

Puchkov stayed silent.

"My life has been defined by war. First the Invasion of Iraq, and then the ongoing war. And now this."

"The Middle East War, Part Three." Puchkov frowned. "Or is it Part Four now?"

Jack snorted, and Puchkov leaned into him, a tiny smile on his lips.

"We've got to do this right." Sobering, Jack rubbed his hands over his face, blinking hard. Nightmares that stole his sleep left him without enough energy to lead the world.

"The UK, Saudi Arabia, and Azerbaijan have agreed to vote yes. Pakistan and The Gambia are voting no." Puchkov listed the countries on his fingers, counting off the votes.

"What about the others?" He and Puchkov were voting *yes*, and with the other three *yes* votes, that brought them to five voting for and two against. They needed nine yes votes, and no veto from China or France.

"Japan is leaning toward yes. They have been asking about our humanitarian aid mission in conjunction with the military operations."

"Offer them a seat at that table."

"Already done. France…" He exhaled, cursing softly. "They are being difficult."

"What else is new?" It was Jack's turn to lean into Puchkov's shoulder, trying to smile.

"They are happy to have nothing to do with this. No soldiers. No money. But they are making demands for their vote."

Jack waited, pinching the bridge of his nose.

"They want to oversee intelligence gathering and want us to agree to allow them to extradite anyone we capture who was involved in the terror attacks on their nation and recommend them to the ICC for prosecution."

Jack tipped his head back, letting it thunk against the heavy oak. 'I'm not opposed to that, but it's going to be difficult to do in any realistic sense. Military operations are not law enforcement."

"It costs nothing to say yes."

"Until we can't deliver on our agreement and they start making life difficult." He shrugged. "Or, more difficult."

"Then we will say they should have sent their policemen in with us, behind our soldiers." Puchkov grinned as Jack chuckled.

"What about Germany? And Egypt?"

"Germany is talking about the refugees. Our mission will likely create more refugees for a short period. Germany is concerned about taking more in. And Egypt is waiting for us to sweeten the deal."

"They want something in exchange for their vote. Figures." He shook his head. "I'll see what the DOD can offer. Maybe some jets. We're upgrading our fleet right now. We could offer them hand-me-downs."

"We are offering something similar. And, for Germany, I will suggest that Russia could help with the economic burden of taking in so many refugees." Puchkov winked. "I know you like it when we feed them."

"It's the humane thing to do, Sergey." He shook his head at Puchkov's almost-playful scoff. "Anything from China?"

If there was one country that could derail their entire proposal, it was China. They could veto the entire resolution as one of the five permanent members of the Security Council, and no matter what the rest of the votes shook out to, a veto would stop everything cold. The other four permanent members seemed set on voting yes, or at least, not vetoing. But China was always an enigma, and ever since the attempted coup in the White House and Colonel Song's quiet aid to Ethan, Lieutenant Cooper, and Faisal, they had been eerily silent on the world stage.

"Nothing. Not a peep. They will speak to no one."

Jack closed his eyes, leaning back against the wall again. "I guess I don't need to ask about Cameroon and Nigeria?"

"No need to ask. Both will vote no. And both delegations have left the discussions."

His foot bounced, heel tapping against the floor. "Do you think Nigeria would have voted yes?"

"I do not waste the thought." Straightening, Puchkov smoothed down his jacket and rolled his neck. "Come, Mr. President. Let's make deals." He held his hand out, bowing his head toward Jack. "Please."

They headed back for the consultation room, shoulders bumping. Puchkov glanced sideways. "You know," he said slowly. "You and Mr. Reichenbach should really come visit Russia. Moscow is beautiful in winter."

Des Moines

Ethan's phone rang in the middle of the night again, buzzing on the pillow next to his head. Fumbling for it, he swiped to answer and dragged it to his ear, eyes closed.

"Hey, baby," he mumbled. "I'm here. It's okay."

Silence. *"Uh. Reichenbach?"*

Shit. He bolted up, clenching his phone hard enough that the case squealed. "Becker?"

He glared at the clock on his nightstand. Three fifty in the morning. "Why are you calling?"

"Another body's been found. And she's got our bills shoved down her throat again. Des Moines PD called me about it."

"Why'd they call you?" Ethan was already moving, going to the closet and grabbing his jeans and boots and sliding on a polo before grabbing his jacket.

"I know a few people on the force. Made some friends. Look, I'm on the way. I was wondering if you... if you'd want to come out."

He could hear the real question beneath Becker's words.

"Yeah. I'm on my way now. Where?"

"I'll send you the address." Becker hesitated. *"When I called—"*

"Shut up," he growled. "I'm on my way."

Flashing blues and reds broke the blackness of the night as Ethan pulled up to the crime scene. He had his own beacon strobing on his dash, and he badged his way through the crime scene tape when a young sheriff's deputy flagged him down.

Snow covered the ground, except for the deep footsteps through the drifts leading to the dumped body. She lay in the snowbank, naked, bruised, and tied up. She'd landed in the snow and hadn't moved, hadn't thrashed. Dumped after death.

A wad of hundreds had been stuffed in her mouth.

Ethan crouched down, peering at her as police and crime scene techs moved around, taking photos and laying out yellow tents, evidence markers on the snow and in the dirt.

"Reichenbach!"

He turned and spotted Becker waving him over to a parked police cruiser. Becker had his notepad on the hood and a female officer stood in the doorway of the cruiser, talking to Becker with bright eyes.

Friends on the force, indeed.

He headed for Becker, dodging CSIs and evidence markers and crunching through the snow. His breath frosted before him, and he tucked his ball cap down over his forehead, trying to hide his face. Like it mattered after Becker shouted his name. But still.

Becker was talking softly with the officer, interviewing her in extraordinary depth about how they'd found the body, what had happened so far, and how their investigation was progressing.

The officer—her nametag read "Walker"—moved off as Ethan approached, her eyes holding Becker's for just a second too long.

Ethan stared at his partner.

"What?" Becker shuffled through his notes.

"Where should I start? You wanting in on the murder investigation, or you sniffing after that cop?"

Becker glared. "Her name is Ellie. She's a good friend. A great cop."

Ethan raised one eyebrow.

"She's out of my league."

"Not sure about that." Ethan shoved his hands into his pockets. "You didn't say anything about wanting in on the murder investigation."

Becker kept his mouth shut. He tapped his notepad against his palm.

"Shepherd warned us off. Told us to stay out of it. We shouldn't even be here. We should be waiting for the official report from the M-E about the bills. Then we can step in."

"And get the door slammed in our faces again? These counterfeit bills are *our* investigation. Someone is counterfeiting *and* murdering—"

"We don't know they're connected."

"We don't know they *aren't*."

Ethan sighed. "I know you want to make a name for yourself. But pissing off the feds isn't the way to do it. Shepherd likes you. Wants to see you go places. You should work with him."

"Goddamn it, Reichenbach. *Jesus*, this must be like a vacation for you, being out here in Nowheresville. But this is the biggest thing to happen in Des Moines for years. You're damn right I want in on it. I want to—"

"Don't you *dare* say this is a vacation for me." Growling, Ethan stepped close to Becker, glowering down at his partner. "Don't you fucking dare."

Becker's eyes went wide. He looked away, his jaw clenching. "There *is* a connection. I know there is," he hissed. "Why would you walk away from that? How is this easy for you?"

"*Nothing* is easy for me," Ethan snapped. "Not a single Goddamn thing." He turned away, blowing out a harsh exhale that fogged in front of him. "I'm just trying not to make anything worse, Becker."

Becker watched him pace, his boots crunching through the snow.

"All right. Look. See if you can get copies of the crime scene report from your friend."

"Won't we get copies? Like last time?"

Ethan shook his head. "The feds want to ice us out of this one. They'll be slow. Real slow."

"I'll ask Ellie."

"We go back to what we can do. We're getting somewhere with Doreen. We're building out her past. Trying to identify her network. We keep going. Work her hard." He glared at Becker, his hands shoved in the pockets of his jacket. "It's not all shoot-outs and firefights. Those are the bad days, Becker. It's the quiet work. Investigation. Preparation. Making sure shit doesn't go wrong."

Becker threw his hand out toward the dumped body. "It's already gone wrong."

"We do what we can do."

Becker wasn't happy, but he stopped arguing, sighed, and closed his notebook. "All right. I'll ask Ellie. She said the FBI is on the way. We should get going."

"Yeah. And before the media, too. I'll see you back at the office."

He stormed off without waiting for Becker's response, shuffling through the snow back to his car.

Luckily, he escaped before the FBI rolled in, and before the media, and he ended up at his cubicle before five in the morning, huddled over a cup of coffee and flipping through the extra reports he'd requested on Doreen. Social Security records. Birth records. Postal records. The places she'd lived.

Becker appeared over his cubicle wall an hour later, dropping a bag of donuts on his desk.

"Hey." Ethan swiveled around and tucked his pencil over his ear. "I found something."

UN Headquarters
New York

The final vote on Jack and Sergey's joint resolution was called Saturday evening, after the sun had set over Manhattan. The ambassadors to the United Nations, their delegates, and the heads of state who were personally representing their nations reentered the Security Council chambers, taking their seats at the semicircular table.

Jack's foot jiggled. He gripped his cell phone in one hand, buried in his lap. Before he'd headed into the council chambers, he'd sent Ethan a quick text. *Voting now.*

His cell buzzed.

[Got the TV on. I see you.]

Jack smiled.

At his side, Puchkov arched one eyebrow as he spied the cell phone in his lap. He snorted softly. "It will be good," he murmured, leaning into Jack's shoulder. "You will both see."

Jack nodded. "We're going to change the world, Sergey. Together." Puchkov slowly smiled and gripped Jack's shoulder.

Azerbaijan's ambassador, the current president of the Security Council, opened the session and spoke quickly about the responsibilities of the chamber and of the nations to secure peace and guide the world toward stability and harmony. He admonished the delegations, calling on them to search their souls for what was in the best interests of the citizens of the world and to let the pettiness in their hearts fall away in the face of humanity's needs.

The voting began.

The nonpermanent members voted first. Azerbaijan cast their vote. *Yes.*

Brazil: *no.* Cameroon: *no.* Egypt: *yes.*

At Jack's side, Puchkov nodded, muttering in Russian.

The Gambia: *no.* Germany: *yes.*

Jack turned his phone over and over in his lap one-handed, the other rolling a pen back and forth between his fingers. He kept his expression schooled, practiced neutrality, though his heart was hammering against his ribs, hard enough to ache.

Japan: *yes*.

Puchkov exhaled.

Nigeria: *no*.

Jack stole a glance sideways at Puchkov. Puchkov stared at the Nigerian delegation, at their president, as if he could wither the man away, turn him to bones and dust with just the force of his glare alone.

Pakistan: *no*.

Swallowing, Jack pressed one hand flat to his notes, spreading out his fingers. The papers grounded him, focused him, as he breathed.

The Saudi Arabian ambassador looked at Jack for a long, silent moment before he voted.

Saudi Arabia: *yes*.

Five *yes* to five *no* for the nonpermanent members. Jack's teeth ground together, and at his side, Puchkov shifted, his first outward sign of nerves. They needed four of the five permanent members to agree, and none to cast a veto.

They had never heard which direction China was leaning.

Azerbaijan gave Jack the first vote, calling for the United States. Jack leaned into the microphone. "Yes, Mr. President." Smiling, he sat back, his tongue pressing hard on the roof of his mouth.

"And the Russian Federation."

"Russia proudly votes yes." Sergey gripped the microphone, angling it toward him, and spoke firmly.

From there, the vote went in historical order. The United Kingdom: *yes*.

Jack inhaled sharply, and Puchkov did the same. One more yes vote was all they needed.

France: *yes*.

Puchkov broke into a wide smile, pounding his fist on the tabletop as Jack pressed his lips together.

There was still one more nation to go. China, with their mercurial nature. Would they blow it all up? Would they veto?

Azerbaijani's president turned to the Chinese delegation. "And China. Your vote, please."

The Chinese ambassador stared at Jack and Puchkov. He said nothing.

And then, he leaned in, speaking in Chinese into the microphone. The translator in Jack's ear provided the translation a second later: "Abstain."

And that was it. Azerbaijan's president couldn't hold back his smile as he pronounced the resolution passed. For the first time in decades, the UN had authorized and supported a global military alliance operation.

Puchkov leaped to his feet, applauding and shaking hands with his advisors, and then reaching for the delegates of the United Kingdom, Germany, and France. Then he turned back to Jack, reaching for his hand.

Jack stood and grasped Puchkov's hand as he beamed. Laughing broadly, Puchkov pulled Jack into a quick hug before holding him at arm's length. "We did it, Jack. We made history."

"We're *making* history, Sergey." Jack gripped Sergey's elbows. "This is just the first step."

His cell phone buzzed in his hands, vibrating against Puchkov's arm. Puchkov's gaze slid to his phone. He smiled.

"Go. You have a phone call to make, I know. We will be speaking to each other much as we prepare, Jack. I will talk to you soon."

Jack gripped his elbows one last time and started extricating himself from the mob of ambassadors and delegates. Daniels and Scott maneuvered him through the crowd. He shared handshakes with the United Kingdom and Germany, and stopped for a longer handshake with the Saudi ambassador. The Gambia, Cameroon, and Nigeria had already stormed out of the council chambers. The Chinese delegation was nowhere to be seen.

Finally, he escaped, heading for the elevators, surrounded by his detail and his staff behind him.

He swiped his phone on.

[I knew you could do it, love. :)]

Jack's heart flip-flopped. He thumbed over Ethan's text, over the word he'd used. *Love.*

Now that was a nickname he could get behind. He smiled again, his cheeks aching, and rolled his top lip between his teeth.

I would have face-planted during my speech if it weren't for your help, love.

[Don't sell yourself short. You're amazing.]

The elevator deposited them at the garage, where Scott had called for the motorcade to wait. They hustled Jack to the SUV as the NYPD met the motorcade at the UN's garage entrance. In moments, sirens blared as they drove through the streets of New York, back to the airport and Washington DC.

Now comes the grueling part. I'm going straight to the Situation Room when I get back. I'll be there for days.

[You'll get that pasty Situation Room tan. ;)]

LOL.

They took FDR up to the Queensboro Bridge, and Jack watched the gray waters of the East River lap at the snowy banks of Queens.

What are you up to?

[Was watching TNN and waiting for the vote. They replayed your speech a dozen times. Other than that, just hanging out in my apartment. Thinking of you.]

Jack bounced in the back of the SUV as they hit a pothole. *Miss you. I wish they'd voted on Thursday.*

The motorcade sped through the streets of Queens, through Astoria, flying through traffic lights. On the streets, cars honked, drivers waved at the SUVs, and people snapped pictures from the sidewalks.

[I'd just be a distraction. You're going to need this time with your staff. You really will be in the Situation Room for days.]

Exhaling, Jack gnawed on his lip again. *Ten days until I see you again.*

[Can't wait, love. :)]

"Mr. President, we'll be arriving at LaGuardia in three minutes."

"Thanks, Scott." Jack grabbed his briefcase and texted Ethan one last time. *About to get to the airport. Text you soon, love.*

[:)]

Seemed their new nickname was sticking. Jack grinned as he shoved his cell into his jacket pocket. He could live with that.

11

Des Moines

"Everybody! In here!" Shepherd's harsh voice broke over the bullpen of Secret Service agents on Monday morning. He waved to his office. "Hurry up!"

Becker fell in beside Ethan. "What now?"

Ethan shrugged.

"Hey." Becker squinted at Ethan. He leaned in, speaking softly as the other agents crowded in beside them. "You didn't go to DC this weekend?"

He shook his head.

Becker frowned, sipping his coffee. When they got to Shepherd's office, Becker moved off, leaning against the windows overlooking the bullpen and leaving Ethan alone on the side wall. A gulf separated him from the other agents; they clustered around the chairs and windows.

"Listen up." Shepherd stood behind his desk, his arms crossed. "You all saw the news from over the weekend. The president is preparing to go to war. While he's in DC, VPOTUS is heading for Chicago to meet privately with the ambassadors from Egypt, Saudi, Jordan, Turkey, and Lebanon. Chicago's office is putting out the call for additional resources. We're sending a team of six agents." He read off four names, and the four called out smiled. Time away from home and protecting the vice president. It would be a treat for many of the guys, a taste of life on the other side of the Secret Service.

"Reichenbach, stay behind. The rest of you, get out of here."

Silently, the rest of the agents filed out. Shepherd stared him down, folding his arms across his chest.

"The vice president has specifically stated that he does *not* want you to be on his detail."

No surprise there. Vice President Green hadn't been the warmest or fuzziest of men, and he'd distanced himself fast and furious from Jack after his and Ethan's relationship had gone public. Ethan stayed quiet.

"But... you're still the most experienced agent in the Midwest region. And Chicago has been specifically ordered to keep these meetings entirely out of the media's spotlight. Which means we need a delicate touch and someone who knows what they're doing managing something that needs to be kept secret."

He didn't know what to say to that.

"So I'm sending you and Becker. Put your case on hold for a week. Becker will work the detail. You're to stay in the command post. Partner with Becker. Help him get his legs underneath him. VPOTUS is operating out of the Ritz up there. You are to go from your hotel room to the command post at the hotel and back to your hotel room. Order room service. I don't want you seen *anywhere*. On the streets, at Starbucks, *anywhere* at all. Got it?"

Ethan looked Shepherd dead in the eyes. "Yes, sir."

"Get going. Tell your partner. You need to be in Chicago by tonight."

The next week passed in a whirlwind.

Ethan grabbed Becker and told him the news, and they left early, heading home to pack for a week in Chicago. Ethan drove back to the office and hopped into Becker's car. Ethan ducked down out of sight of the reporters as they made their way out of town.

When they got to Chicago, Becker checked them both into the hotel, and with his head down and ball cap pulled low, Ethan lugged his duffel to his room, connected to Becker's with a slip door.

They headed for the command post after that, set up in one of the hotel's conference rooms. Becker was like a puppy let loose for the first time, wide-eyed and taking in everything. His first protective detail. His first taste of the other side.

Other agents weren't as thrilled with the assignment, or with Ethan's presence. In the command post, eyes slid sideways, lingering on him.

They got their rotational assignments and their radios and headed back for their rooms, where Becker talked Ethan's ear off while they sipped beers from the minifridge. How cool the command post was. What the different ambassadors were going to be like.

Ethan didn't have the heart to stop him.

He and Jack Skyped late that night, both too tired for a long conversation. But Jack smiled and blew Ethan a kiss, a simple ritual that had become the foundation of his nightly routine. Ethan went to sleep with a smile on his face.

Each day, the newspapers dissected Jack's actions in the White House, prognosticating and pontificating on what his and the generals' battle plans were likely to be, and how close he and President Puchkov were becoming. In Chicago, Ethan sat in the command post and listened to Becker grouse about the rude delegations and the boredom of the detail as the vice president and the nations' ambassadors ensconced themselves in discussions for hours.

"*This sucks*," Becker breathed into his mic, keyed to a private channel for Ethan. "*How the hell did you do this for twelve years?*"

"It helps when the protectees are better people." Becker snorted, completely undignified.

"*For those of us who aren't looking to bang the protectee, do you have any other advice for how to make this less soul-crushing? I swear I can see the paint peeling off the wall.*"

Ethan chuckled into his coffee cup. "Welcome to protections, Becker."

"*Is this what it's like at the White House?*"

"No." Ethan leaned back in his chair, glancing around the dark command post. The lights were dim, most of the room's illumination coming from computer monitors and laptops open on long lines of tables set up in rows. It was the middle of the night. Ethan and Becker were holding down the overnight shift again. "At least, not most of the time. There's always so much going on, between the president's daily schedule, visitors, special events, and then travel. There's always a thousand things to take care of. And DC—and the White House—is usually keyed up and extra anal, anyway—"

Becker snorted again.

"—so there's usually not enough time for boredom."

"*Well, this sucks,*" Becker said softly. "*The ambassador has six escorts in the hotel suite with him. Sometimes I can hear them.*" Something that sounded like Becker shuddering floated over the line. "*Between that and this very empty and boring hallway, I think I'd actually rather be back in Des Moines chasing down counterfeiters.*"

Ethan grinned. "What? Financial crimes not high-speed enough for you?"

A long sigh as Becker deflated. "*I wanted to work my way up to something. Something... badass. Meaningful. Like what you did. The presidential detail. Man...*"

Ethan's heart clenched.

"*But...I'm not sure anymore.*" Becker sounded off. Dejected, and something else. "*Maybe I'm in the wrong agency. I mean, what's going on in there, with the ambassador, isn't even really legal, and I'm a sworn agent. This is messed up.*"

"Happens all the time. Sad to say." Ethan leaned forward, balancing on his elbows as he hovered over his coffee. "Every year, we all hear about the stories from the agents detailed to New York for the UN General Assembly. Our guys provide detail protection for all the heads of state who come in. What they do when they're here..." Ethan shook his head. "But there's a lot of good in the job, too. We make a real difference. Every day should be boring if we're doing our job right. Everything should be controlled. Stable. Safe. And everyone is relying on you to deliver that. Everyone, not just your protectee. The whole world counts on us to keep our people safe. Doing that right... There's a lot of meaning in that."

"Sounds like you miss it."

I miss Jack. "Yeah," he grunted. "But, you know. This is what it is."

Silence, again, heavy with Becker's unasked questions.

"Gross," Becker hissed. *"Ugh, I can hear the ambassador going at it. And the girls are obviously faking."*

Ethan chuckled.

"Dude, quick, tell me some stories. Block out these sounds. Gotta help me out here, man. That's what partners are for, right?"

Grinning, Ethan launched into a story of him and Scott pranking Daniels at the White House. And then the Easter Egg Roll when Scott had pulled the short straw and had to dress up as the Easter Bunny. The time he'd slipped one of Jack's predecessors a glass of vodka instead of a glass of water during his holiday photo line, and the mischievous smile the president had given him in return. Hours later, the president was as red-faced as Santa Claus, but he was having the time of his life, and so were his guests. Days spent in training at Rowley, running counterattack scenarios in the motorcade with the special tactics squads, breaching drills, counterterrorism exercises, and simulating the worst day in the world for a Secret Service agent: their protectee coming under attack.

"Was it anything like training when it did happen?" Becker interrupted softly. *"In Ethiopia?"*

"No." Ethan's voice choked off and his throat clenched. "But that's on me. Because—" He swallowed. "Because in training, you're distant. And in Ethiopia, I already loved him." Silence. He didn't need to say more. The training both he and Becker had been through had emphasized, over and over again, how important distance was between them and their protectees. How any personal attachments could be the difference between success and failure. Objectivity blown, what choices would a compromised agent make? What hesitations, or rash decisions, would be made, and who would pay the price when it all came apart?

Ethan's throat stayed tight, memories and pain hammering him hard. Ethiopia had been desperation and bitten-off prayers, doing everything he could to get Jack out alive. His objectivity had been shattered, and he hadn't cared if he'd lived or died.

"*When I called that night...*" Becker trailed off. "*Who did you think I was?*"

"Who do you think?"

Shuffling. "*The ambassador is finishing up. Finally,*" Becker grumbled. "*I need to get these girls down and out the service entrance.*"

"I'll send a team to meet you at the elevator." Ethan switched over to the main comms channel and routed a waiting team to Becker. No one talked back to him over the open net, but there was a little too much hesitation, a little too much dead air, between his tasking and their acknowledgement.

Ethan listened to Becker herd the escorts out of the hotel, and Becker falling in with the other agents in the ready room. No one talked to Ethan for the rest of the night.

They were cut loose from Chicago after the vice president and all the ambassadors had left for the airport. Other agents stuck around to help break down the command post and close up shop with the Chicago agents, but not them. Ethan hung in the background, standing apart from the crowd of agents filling the briefing room, and Becker traded business cards and handshakes as he made his goodbyes.

Ethan waited in the car for Becker, his ball cap on, until Becker threw his suitcase in the back seat and clambered into the front. A few of the other agents had invited Becker out for beers, and Ethan had been prepared to hang out in the back of the command post for a few hours, fending off glares and stares. But, Becker had declined.

"Didn't want to go out with the guys?"

"Want to get back to work on our case." Becker chewed at his thumbnail as he squinted. "There's a murderer out there."

"Yeah, but that's not our lane." Ethan drove out of the parking lot, eyebrows arched behind his shades. "You heard Shepherd. We're running the counterfeiting side. The FBI is handling the murders." And, though counterfeiting was a crime, their entire investigation could be put on hold to go to Chicago for the week and backfill the protective detail for the vice president. The Secret Service had its priorities.

"But you found something on Doreen." Becker rolled his head to the side and fixed Ethan with a glare. "And we can use that to get more out of her. Something the FBI hasn't been able do. And, if we get back early, we could go interrogate her before you have to go."

"Go?"

"To the airport. It's Friday." Becker stared like Ethan had lost his mind. "You're going to DC, aren't you?"

Ethan shook his head.

Becker's scowl deepened. He turned in his seat, straightening as he stared at Ethan's profile. "You didn't go last weekend. And you're not going this weekend. I thought all of that crap they print about you guys was garbage, but—" He squinted. "I mean, you knew every word of his speech."

Ethan ditched his ball cap into the back seat. "The UN vote stole one weekend. And I'm not going this weekend because I'm using my vacation days for Christmas. I've been using half days every Friday for three months. And I lost a bunch, after—" He shrugged. "I want to have more time with him over the holiday. So, I'm going on Wednesday instead."

Whistling, Becker shook his head. "No special treatment, huh?"

"I don't want any." Ethan shot him a glare. "Neither of us want special treatment."

"So… You guys are good?" Becker's face scrunched up. "What everyone is saying. What they're printing. It's all crap, right?"

Ethan's gaze met Becker's through his shades. This kid, this man almost half his age, his unwanted partner and supposed babysitter, was staring at him, his worry and wonder and hesitation all mixing together. "Yeah," he said softly. *Right now, at least.*

Relief flitted across Becker's face, but he played it off, leaning back in his seat. "That's cool," he said, propping one arm up on the doorframe. "You guys look pretty good in that photo you've got hidden on your desk."

"Thanks." He didn't really know what else to say. He just kept his eyes on the road.

"I mean, it's got to be something real—something serious—if you were willing to risk everything for the guy. You're pretty strict, so—" Becker's head bobbed back and forth. "And I don't know the guy, but the president seems like a cool dude." He shrugged.

Ethan's eyes flicked sideways. Becker was on a roll.

"Seems like the kind of guy who doesn't do assholes, you know? I totally thought you were a jerk, at first—"

He couldn't keep it in. Ethan snorted and burst out laughing, loud chuckles that made him shake. His cheeks burned.

"What?" Becker glared. "You were That Guy who broke every rule and then kissed the president on the White House lawn. We all thought you'd be a *prick*. Demanding, arrogant, think you're all that—"

"Not that part." Ethan shook his head, still smirking. "What you said before that."

"The president doesn't do assholes? Yeah, he seems like a guy that wouldn't put up with—"

Becker stopped dead. Turned fourteen different shades of magenta, flushing from tomato red to fuchsia and back again. His lips clamped shut and he glared out the passenger window.

Ethan laughed again.

"I take it back. You are a fucking jerk."

"You said it. Not me."

He was still grinning when his phone buzzed. Ethan fished it out, keeping one eye on the empty highway ahead of him as he swiped his phone on and saw a message from Jack flash up. *My VP is back from Chicago. Will you be home in time for our call?*

[Driving. Can you talk?]

His phone rang a few seconds later. Ethan glanced at Becker, still glaring out the window.

"Hey, love."

Becker's spine went rigid, his shoulders taut.

"*Hey.*" There was a smile in Jack's voice, light and bright. "*Just wanted to check in with you. See if we were on for our usual call time tonight or if you had to do anything else in Chicago.*"

"We're good. Driving back now. We were cut loose when Green went to the airport."

"*Sounds good.*"

"How's camping in the Situation Room going? Have you worked through the entire takeout menu yet?"

Becker turned, staring at Ethan like Ethan had lost his mind.

Jack laughed. "*Almost. We ordered Thai three times. It was a room favorite. But it's going well. Green did all right with his part. I think we're on track. And, everything is going well with Russia, too.*"

"I can't believe President Puchkov is being so friendly toward you. Think it's real?" Ethan could see the whites ringing Becker's eyes.

"*I hope so. I'm enjoying getting to know the man. I might actually like him.*"

Ethan laughed. "I'm sure it's all an FSB ploy. He's trying to *make* you like him."

"*Maybe.*" That smile in Jack's voice was back. "*But I'm going to hope for the best.*"

"You always do."

"*Oh, the stewards were asking. They couldn't find your tux. Is it in my closet? Or does Agent Collard know where it is?*"

"If they haven't cleaned out my locker in Horsepower, my tux is down there. Ask Scott. He can get it, if it's there. If not, he's got a key to my condo."

"*I'll ask. And, do you want to do matching bowties for the Christmas Ball?*"

"Matching *black* bowties?"

"Matching Christmas bow ties." Jack's voice was teasing. *"Santa and reindeer? Or snowmen?"*

Laughing, Ethan shook his head. "Your staff would never let you wear that. Remember what they said about your yellow tie?"

"But you said it made me look presidential."

"A reindeer bowtie will not make you look presidential, love. Sorry to say." He pretended to sigh, watching out of the corner of his eye as Becker's jaw dropped.

Jack was laughing, though. *"All right, matching black bow ties. I'll have to come up with something else we can do together."*

"Matching nose rings."

Jack snorted.

Becker shook his head, fighting back a smile. He looked away. "With jingle bells."

"Oh, something with bells." That teasing tone was back in Jack's voice. Then he sighed. *"I'm going to miss you tonight."*

Ethan's throat clenched, and the humor of the moment fled. "Me too." Fridays were supposed to be the good days.

"Maybe we could Skype more over the weekend?"

"Yeah. We should. I'm not doing anything except laundry."

"Why doing laundry? You don't need to wear anything when you're here."

Ethan barked out a laugh, his cheeks warming. He glanced at Becker, wondering if the volume was up enough for Becker to hear Jack's voice.

Becker was resolutely staring out the window, but his shoulders were shaking up and down.

"Uh, I'd say something similar, but I'm not alone right now."

"Sorry." Jack didn't sound sorry at all.

"Don't be, love."

Jack didn't say anything, but the soft sigh, the warm happiness he exuded, flowed over the phone.

"I'll talk to you soon."

"Love you."

Ethan's eyes darted to Becker. "Love you too."

He hung up, and the miles rolled on, asphalt humming beneath their tires. Becker kept staring out the window, not looking at Ethan until they stopped for gas. Ethan pumped while Becker went inside. He came out a few minutes later with two bottles of water and two candy bars.

Becker tossed over a bottle of water and said, "I'll drive for a while, if you want to text and stuff."

12

Des Moines

Monday morning just before dawn, Ethan and Becker strode into the jail, each holding a steaming cup of coffee, and badged into the interrogation rooms. The same sheriff who had been in the room when Ethan had lost his cool was there, and he nodded to Ethan once, almost smiling.

They waited together for the sheriff to bring Doreen out from her cell.

"Good weekend?" Becker was twitchy, adrenaline and excitement making his toes tap against the tile floor.

Ethan nodded. He and Jack had texted most of Saturday while Jack was playing catch-up with his core staff, dealing with domestic issues from Congress that had backed up while he was working on the invasion plans with his Joint Chiefs and Puchkov's envoys. Sunday, they kept Skype on while they watched football together, laughing and joking as they lounged around on their couches, a thousand miles apart. It wasn't like being there and holding Jack in his arms, but it was better than being on his own with just his swirling thoughts and aching heart.

"Bet you're ready for Wednesday, huh?" Becker tipped back in his chair, balancing it on two legs.

"Jack keeps saying we need a time machine."

"Shit, just have him call Area 51. I'm sure they'll hook him up. I mean, there's got to be *some* perks to dating the president."

Ethan snorted as the door opened, and the sheriff escorted a grumpy, bedraggled Doreen into the room. She shuffled, glaring through her stringy hair hanging in front of her face, and collapsed into the chair opposite them with a grunt. She yawned through the sheriff securing her cuffs to the floor and the table, and tipped her head forward, trying to go back to sleep.

Becker quirked one eyebrow at Ethan. His eyes sparkled. Time for Ethan to hit it home.

"Good morning, Gabriela."

She stiffened, every muscle in her body going taut. Her sleepiness, her practiced indifference, vanished from one moment to the next. She stayed still, her hair hanging in front of her face, but it was the wariness of a cornered animal that kept her frozen.

"I thought Doreen was an unusual name for you from the first time we met. Too old. But, then again, old names are what you're left with when you are using a fake identity."

Slowly, so slowly that Ethan could practically hear her bones creak, Gabriela sat up, rolling her head until she was staring at Ethan, wide-eyed from behind her curtain of lank hair.

"Let me know if I got it all right. You were a young teen and you wanted a new start. Maybe your home life was crap. Maybe you were escaping a gang. Or drugs. Or your parents were beating you. Or a boyfriend who wasn't worth jack shit. You did some research online. Found out you could take over a dead baby's identity pretty easily in some parts of America. Rural parts. So you wandered through cemeteries until you found a headstone for Doreen Watts in Platte, South Dakota. Doreen died when she was one and a half. There were no records online. The death certificate was filed with the local church. No Social Security number was ever issued. From a governmental standpoint, you picking up where she left off would look practically seamless."

Gabriela didn't move. Barely breathed.

"So you got your driver's license with Doreen's birth certificate in Sioux Falls. Moved around. Fell in with the wrong crowd." Ethan shrugged, crossing one leg over the other. "How am I doing so far?"

"You don't know anything about me," Gabriela said, her voice low, almost growling. "You don't know a damn thing."

"Why don't you tell me, then? Explain it to me."

Silence. Gabriela swallowed, slowly.

"You're in here waiting for your trial on counterfeiting charges, Gabriela. You're looking at up to ten years in federal prison. We can add felony identity theft to this, and—" Ethan whistled. He shook his head, his lips pursed. "That's a long time in prison."

She sniffed, and her fingers curled into her hands. She trembled.

"What were you running from?" Becker said softly.

"Fuck you!" Gabriela exploded. "You have no idea what you're talking about! No fucking idea! You've never had it hard! Ever!" She tried to back away, run away from them, but the chain fixing her cuffs to the table pulled her up short. She collapsed instead, curling into herself and sobbing as she doubled over in the chair.

Ethan stayed quiet. So did Becker.

After a few minutes, Ethan pulled out a few napkins he'd stuffed into his coat pocket from the coffee shop. He stood and walked to Gabriela's side, kneeling and holding them under the curtain of her hair. She glared but took the napkins, wiping at her wet eyes and running nose.

"I know what it's like to lose," he said softly. "Lose… everything. And have to face up to things you've done."

"I wouldn't change anything I did," Gabriela snapped. "I'm a survivor."

"I wouldn't change what I did either. But I still understand."

Gabriela sniffed, long and loud.

"We can help you, Gabriela. You're part of something—something bigger than just these faked bills. You're connected to the two dead girls we've found. They had the bills you forged on them when they died." Ethan stood and walked back to his chair. Becker gave him a tight smile and a barely-there nod. "What can you tell us about those girls?"

She sniffed again, but sat up a bit, rolling the soaked napkins in her hands as she stared at the floor. "You're right about a lot of it. But not the why. Me and those other girls… We came across the border together. Paid a coyote a grand each to get us across the border."

Ethan and Becker shared a long look. A coyote, a human smuggler working the southern border, usually took people across for far more than a thousand dollars each.

"And then?" Becker leaned forward.

Gabriela shifted, biting her lip. "We had to pay more, he said, when we got here. Had to earn our way." She gestured weakly up and down her body.

Ethan's eyes slipped closed. How young had she been, forced to prostitute herself, locked in the clutches of a human trafficker?

"She got us out." Suddenly, Gabriela was on fire, her eyes blazing, staring at them with fury and passion in her eyes. "She saved us. Got us away from those *pinche putos*!" She spat, lobbing a wad of spit to the floor.

"Who?"

"Mother," Gabriela breathed. "Mother. She saved us all. Helped us get our new names. Helped us hide. And, yeah, she's the one who taught me to make those fake Benjamins. But—" Her lips clamped shut, as if she was physically restraining herself from going any further.

"But?" Becker prodded.

Gabriela fought with herself, her lips twisting, nose sniffling. Her whole body shook. Her feet tapped on the floor and she gnawed on her fingers. "But I left her," Gabriela finally whispered. "And now my sisters are dead."

Pitching forward, her tears started again, raining from Gabriela's eyes and into her palms. The jumpsuit sleeves, too long for her, slid down her forearms, covering the scars of her needle tracks and slipping over her bony wrists, almost covering her hands pressed over her face. For a moment, she looked like the frightened young teen she must have been, scared and alone and bereft.

This woman—Mother—kept coming up. Their link in the counterfeiting chain, and now, the missing link in the murdered girls. She was part of the FBI's locked files, behind their iron curtain of refusal to share intelligence.

"Who is Mother, Gabriela?" Ethan leaned forward, trying to close the distance across the table, trying to reach for her. "Who is she?"

Gabriela's head shook, left and right and back again, as if it hurt. "I *can't*," she whispered. "I *can't*." Sniffing, she stared Ethan down, licking her lips. "You ever love someone so much you'll die for them? Do anything for them? Even if it means you're done for?"

Next to Ethan, Becker stiffened.

Ethan held her watery gaze. "Yes."

"Then you know why I can't say anything to you."

They kept Gabriela's interrogation to themselves.

They never recorded their meetings. They didn't file it in the system. Didn't write up a report on it. Didn't do anything that would get the attention of the FBI.

"Trust me?" Ethan asked Becker. "I've got an idea. For when I'm in DC. I'll let you know what happens when I'm back."

Becker nodded and dropped the issue completely.

Wednesday finally arrived.

Starting on Monday, Jack had sent countdown selfies every few hours, growing more exuberant with each. Wednesday morning Ethan woke up to a selfie of Jack lying back in bed, completely naked except for a Santa hat perched on his crotch, sporting a wide, wicked grin.

Ethan didn't have a single decoration in his apartment and couldn't respond in kind, but he sent back a teasing message after he picked his jaw up off the floor. *[Is Santa looking for a helper?]*

Yep. But not a little one. ;)

[Oh, trust me. It's not little. Esp not after that...]

:)

Ethan headed to the office for the morning to review case notes for another of Becker's cases. Every hour, his phone buzzed with another text from Jack.

Five more hours.

Ethan grinned. *[Are you getting anything done today?]*

Absolutely not. Lawrence is ready to throw a fit. :)

LOL

Becker said his name for the third time, and Ethan jumped. He grinned guiltily and tapped out a final message. *I'm not getting anything done either.*

Another hour passed.

His phone buzzed.

Ethan was alone in his cube, and he swiped his phone on and found a selfie of Jack at his desk, eyes blazing with joy, trying to hold back a smile as he took a surreptitious selfie from the vantage of his lap. *Four more hours!!*

[I don't want to know what meeting you're doing this in, do I?]

Nothing gives me more pleasure than to text you while the congressional leadership that's lambasting me drones on and on...

[Nothing? :) *]*

Well... :)

"You guys are disgusting."

Ethan startled, spinning in his chair, and found Becker standing behind him, shaking his head and reading over Ethan's shoulder. Becker was buttoned up in his wool overcoat and had his scarf around his neck.

"Going to lunch?" Ethan stood, pocketing his cell and reaching for his coat. It was time for him to head out as well.

"Wondered if you wanted a ride to the airport? Maybe the press won't follow my car."

"Yeah. Thanks."

They headed out together, Shepherd watching them both from his office like a hawk. Ethan ducked down in Becker's front seat, and the press watched their car slip out of the parking garage. No one followed. Ethan popped up once they hit the highway, and Becker grinned. The sky was winter gray, but the snow was holding back, and they drove quickly, listening to the radio belt out Des Moines's rock hits.

At the airport, Becker dropped Ethan at the curb, blessedly free from the media, and waved from the car. "Text me when you're going to get back. I'll pick you up."

"Thanks, man. Happy holidays."

"You too. Have a good time with... you know." Becker shrugged, smiled, and then drove off.

Ethan's shadow appeared as he was waiting in line at the airport coffee shop, and he bought his shadow's coffee again, throwing in a gift card for the barista to tape to his cup when he picked it up from the counter. Ethan headed for the gate, whistling under his breath, and pulled out his phone.

[You kept that Santa hat, right?]

A few minutes passed, and then Jack sent back a picture of him at his desk in the Oval Office, Santa hat perched on his head.

Ethan closed his eyes, fighting his body's reaction and his grin. He didn't know how to respond, so he snapped a red-faced selfie and sent it back.

I think you should wear the Santa hat when you get here.

[Okay]

And *only* the Santa hat. :)

A zing went through Ethan's body, singeing his bones. Jack's open desire of him—his body, his unbridled masculinity—made his world spin dizzily. There was no way anyone could ever mistake Ethan for being feminine, and Jack's embrace of that—of who Ethan was—made him feel desired like nothing else ever had. Jack *wanted* him. All of him.

Grinning, Ethan typed back *[Deal! :)]* as the call for boarding began. He slipped onboard first, settling into his window seat in first class, and kept joking with Jack until everyone else had boarded and they were ready for takeoff.

Jack's last text came in before he turned off his phone. *Two more hours!!!!!!!*

The media, tipped off about his imminent arrival, was out in force at Dulles airport when Ethan landed. He pushed through the throng of reporters to his designated pickup location.

Scott was waiting at the curb, his hands in the pockets of his wool trench coat, stone-faced and solemn. Snow lightly fell, settling on his shoulders, and he looked, to the world, grim.

Ethan spotted the light in his eyes, though, a slight twinkle as he winked when Ethan got near. "Don't cream yourself," Scott muttered into Ethan's ear as he opened the rear door for him.

Frowning, Ethan slid inside—

And found Jack sitting there, against the window and just out of sight of the hounding media, beaming. "Hi," Jack breathed.

Scott shoved the door closed on Ethan before any of the photographers spotted Jack. Scott hopped into the front and the driver took off, all while Ethan stared speechlessly at Jack.

"What are you doing here?" he finally said, speaking around his own wide smile. "It's the middle of the afternoon. Don't you have more important things to do?"

"Nothing more important than this." Jack reached for him, sliding his hand up Ethan's arm, cupping the back of his neck. He pulled, gently dragging Ethan across the back seat as he lunged for him.

They met in the middle, lips tangling. Ethan shucked his duffel to the floorboards and reached for Jack, threading his fingers through Jack's hair, cradling his face and running his hands down his neck, his shoulders.

Jack moaned and grabbed Ethan's coat. A moment later, he shoved it back, pushing it down Ethan's shoulders.

And then Ethan shoved Jack's suit jacket off and tugged at his tie, and Jack melted back on the black leather seat, his legs spreading. Ethan followed, pressing his body against Jack's until they were a mess of arms and legs and an endless kiss, humping each other as they frantically worked at buttons and zippers, trying to get hands on skin.

Jack wrapped his hand around Ethan's cock first, and Ethan groaned into Jack's neck as Jack pumped him hard and fast. He had the top buttons of Jack's shirt undone, but not his tie, and he pressed kisses around the yellow silk as he humped Jack's hand and thigh.

He bumped Jack's hand off, though, and fumbled at Jack's fly until he had his hard cock out and in his hands. Ethan folded himself down, ass almost pressed to the blacked-out window as he kneeled on the seat and swallowed Jack's cock.

Jack cursed and slapped a hand against the privacy glass partition separating them from the front, and Scott and his driver. The other threaded through Ethan's hair.

Jack let him suck for a few minutes. He tugged at Ethan's shoulders, pulling him back up until they were awkwardly pressed together, legs crammed in the floorboards and on the seats, hips rocking, jackets tangled on their arms, ties askew and shirts partially unbuttoned. Their hips met, and their cocks, and both moaned as they pressed together, kissing and never stopping as the SUV zoomed back to the White House.

Until the intercom overhead buzzed and Scott's voice broke through the SUV. "*We're arriving in two minutes, Mr. President.*"

They froze. Ethan stared down at Jack—lips swollen and red, hair fucked beyond belief, clothes more off than on, cock raging hard and dark purple, rising from his suit pants.

Jack grinned. He thrust his hips up once, rolling into Ethan. Ethan shuddered. Jack reached for the intercom switch. "Take us to the underground entrance, Agent Collard. If you please."

A long, silent moment. Jack watched Ethan as Ethan counted down the seconds until they were back at the White House.

"*Respectfully, Mr. President,*" Scott buzzed back. "*No shit.*"

Jack burst out laughing. Ethan leaned down, biting his nipple through his undershirt as Jack shouted, and then the SUV turned down a ramp, into the White House garage. They finally sat up and tried to sort out their clothes and hair as Scott's driver made the slowest approach ever to the underground entrance.

When Scott opened the back door, Ethan slid out, holding his duffel in front of his lap. His tie was loose, the top of his shirt partially unbuttoned, and he'd lost his jacket. Scott snorted.

Jack followed, and Scott turned purple trying to hold back his laughter. Jack's hair was standing straight up, his shirt was untucked and mostly unbuttoned, revealing his white undershirt, his tie was undone and hanging in a long line around his neck, and he had Ethan's jacket folded over his arms, hanging in front of his crotch and hiding his cock.

He also had the most innocent expression on his face, something sweet and simple, which made the whole thing ten times worse.

The agents holding post at the entrance chuckled as Ethan and Jack breezed past and onto the service elevator that would take them straight to the Residence, bypassing the public spaces of the White House.

Ethan and Jack stood side by side, three feet apart, and waited for the elevator doors to close.

Jack smiled serenely, as if nothing were amiss. Ethan coughed. Outside the elevator, Scott grinned at them both, shaking his head.

The doors shut.

Ethan dropped his duffel like it was on fire. Jack flung his jacket to the ground. They crashed into each other, meeting in the middle of the elevator, but Ethan backed Jack up until he hit the wall, his hands running over Jack's body. Moaning, Jack tipped his head back, and he snaked one leg around Ethan's.

Ethan kneaded Jack's ass. Jack shuddered, and he wrapped his arms around Ethan's neck and jumped, both legs going around Ethan's hips. Ethan pressed him against the elevator wall, driving his hard cock against Jack's, grinding them together. Jack's thighs squeezed, and his fingers ran through Ethan's hair.

"Can you carry me like this?" Jack breathed into his ear.

"Fuck yes," Ethan nipped at Jack's jaw. His hands squeezed Jack's ass again.

"Do it." Jack tugged at Ethan's tie, pulling it off, throwing it on the floor. His fingers worked the buttons of Ethan's shirt as he rolled his hips into Ethan's. "Take me to bed. I want you. Ethan—"

Ethan's lips found Jack's just as the elevator door opened to the Residence. Ethan carried Jack down the hall as Jack cupped his face, kissing him nonstop until Ethan laid Jack on the bed and knelt on all fours over him.

They stripped in record time, clothes and shoes flying every which way. Ethan kissed down Jack's body as each piece came off, swallowing Jack when his cock was free.

Jack kicked out of his pants and boxers and spread his legs wide. "Lower, Ethan," Jack breathed.

Ethan froze. His eyes darted up. Met Jack's gaze.

Jack swallowed. "Please. I want—" His voice broke off.

Never. Never before had they gone near Jack's ass. It had been a no-go zone, his entrance something Ethan—and Jack—had shied away from. Jack seemed to enjoy topping, and Ethan had finally understood what he'd heard for years: that, somewhere, there was a top who could convince him to be a bottom.

What was this, then?

There was something lining Jack's eyes, buried in his gaze as he stared down at Ethan. Hunger, lust, and need, but also determination. And—just faintly—uncertainty. Fear, even.

Slow. Ethan had always said slow to Jack. And he'd meant it, every word, every time. If Jack wanted to explore more, go further with his own body, then they'd go slow there, too.

Ethan pressed his hands to Jack's thighs, gently holding him back, and leaned in. He held Jack's stare until he couldn't, and with the first press of his lips, of his tongue lower than Jack's balls, Jack flung one arm over his face and moaned.

Ethan nudged one of Jack's legs farther up until it was against Jack's chest and pressed his tongue over Jack's hole, and then inside.

Jack's head hit the mattress, his back arching, his muscles going rigid. Ethan kept up, soft nibbles and gentle sucks mixed with the long press and stroke of his tongue. He moaned, vibrating against

Jack as he pressed deeper, stroking, and he ended up twisting Jack's hips and diving deeper until his face was buried almost entirely between his ass cheeks. One thumb kept stroking just behind Jack's balls, steady pressure against his prostate. Jack finally relaxed completely beneath Ethan. He reached down for him, fingers trembling as they stroked through Ethan's hair.

Everything about Jack was shivering, a quivering, raw nerve, and Ethan's world was nothing but a static-filled hum, Jack's pants, his whispered pleas, and the taste of his body. Musk, sweat, and Jack, something that Ethan could never describe. Just him.

"Ethan," Jack breathed. His back bowed, arching taut, and his fingers gripped Ethan's hair. "What's— What are you—"

He pressed behind Jack's balls and slipped his tongue inside him, as far as it could go, and felt Jack fly apart. Jack screamed, shuddering beneath Ethan's fingers, his mouth, coming hard, his whole body jerking as long lines of come roped over his chest. One hand flew to his cock, grabbing and stroking himself through the aftershocks.

Ethan was up on his knees in an instant, jerking himself furiously as he hovered over Jack and leaned in, kissing him like he wouldn't ever stop. In moments, his come painted Jack's stomach and chest as Jack's trembling hands stroked up his sides and over his shoulders.

He collapsed after, face-planting into Jack's shoulder and the mattress.

Jack panted, but then chuckled and stared down at his come-covered body.

"Wow," Jack breathed. "That was…"

Ethan swallowed. Too much? Had he gone too far? "Okay?" Ethan kissed Jack's neck and his pounding pulse.

"Beyond okay. Way, way beyond okay." Jack rolled, wrapping his arms and legs around Ethan and nuzzled his cheek, grinning. "Let's do that again."

13

White House

They were late for their own Christmas Ball later that evening.

Scott hollered from the landing for Ethan to quit delaying the president as Ethan helped fix Jack's tux and retie his bowtie. Jack was trying to style his hair again, mussed by Ethan's hands after pushing Jack up on the bathroom counter and blowing him in his tux.

Jack kissed Ethan hard and then jogged down the main hall to join Scott at the top of the Grand Staircase while Ethan headed down the hall in the other direction, back toward the service elevator.

Ethan heard Jack ask Scott, "How do I look?" and Scott sigh in response.

Outside the elevator, Ethan's duffel, jacket, and tie lay, delivered to them from where they'd left it all behind. Ethan's cheeks burned as he stepped over the pile. If he had to guess, it would have been Scott. His friend had probably waited at the elevator in the underground garage, checking to make sure they *hadn't* done exactly what they *had* done.

Jack came down the stairs and made his solo entrance for the media while Ethan met up with Hanier and Caldwell in the basement. Both were grinning, and Ethan's face burned again. He'd almost forgotten how fast the White House gossip chain moved. No doubt, every agent on the detail had heard of their arrival. It was probably screen-capped from the security videos, too, and posted down in Horsepower.

They waited awhile, chatting in the basement before winding their way up the rear steps and slipping into the East Room after Jack's photo line had begun. This was his second and last photo line for the year, the first having been at the Hanukkah Festival of Lights Jack had hosted the week before while Ethan was in Chicago.

Guests stretched in a long line, waiting for their turn with Jack in front of the glittering Christmas tree beside the gold-bedecked mantel. Secret Service agents flanked Jack on all sides, one holding purses and phones for the guests while they stepped up to Jack for handshakes and smiling photos. Daniels shepherded the people through, and Scott stayed just off Jack's shoulder, watching everyone and everything. Welby hung back, and another, younger agent ran water and the occasional glass of champagne for Jack. Marine Corps guards in full dress rounded out the tableau.

Ethan stayed on the other side of the East Room, sipping his own champagne and listening to the band play soft big-band-style Christmas carols. A few couples were dancing, and others who had already had their photo with Jack were milling around the banquet stations. Waiters mingled with glasses of champagne and wine. Secret Service agents dotted the walls and exits. Ethan hung back, chatting with Keifer and Beech while the photo line wore on.

It was the first time he had ever been a guest at the Christmas Ball. Usually he was standing side by side with Scott, ushering people through the photo line and slipping the president—before Jack, at least—some vodka tonics. It was strange—and a little bit lonely—to be across the room with no official duty, just watching Jack.

Jack sought him out, though, sending Ethan a wink.

Candles were lit along the walls, flickering off sconces and reflecting in the huge mirrors hanging on the brocade walls. Golden light spun from the decorations, twinkling over the room. Silver snowflakes twirled lazily overhead, and spruce and cranberry hung in the air.

Ethan nearly broke his champagne flute when the next person in the photo line stepped up to Jack. He watched Jack's spine straighten, his shoulders clench, but Jack pasted on his polite smile and posed for a photo. He held his hands clasped in front of him, though.

"Amazing, isn't it?" Beech leaned in. "Who shows up to these things."

Ethan grunted, his eyes glaring daggers into Senator Stephen Allen, the self-proclaimed leader of the Republicans in Congress mounting political—and increasingly personal—attacks against Jack.

Jack nodded to the senator and Daniels ushered him away before Senator Allen could get his hand out for a handshake. Ethan caught Jack flash a quick glance his way, a quirk of his eyebrows, before he welcomed the next guests, a family of four with two little girls in matching red velvet dresses.

His heart clenched as he watched Jack kneel down and talk with the young girls. They were five, maybe six years old. Adorable, with round, dark cheeks and springy curls and shy smiles. Jack laughed as one hid behind her mother's gold dress, and then he posed with the family and shook both the mom and dad's hands.

Did Jack want children? Had he ever wanted that for himself? Ethan had never given children a second thought. Would Jack want a family, though? Was that something that could, eventually, pull Jack away—

Enough. Ethan gulped down more champagne and turned back to watching the crowds. More people were dancing and the din in the room had grown.

He got lost talking to some of the other agents and a few White House staffers he had known and befriended. He skirted the press and the photographers who kept trying to get near.

Suddenly, Jack was speaking into his ear. "Hey beautiful."

Ethan spun, almost dropping his champagne flute. He was hiding out by the windows and the third Christmas tree, and he hadn't seen Jack approach. Beyond, Scott and Welby were keeping a slight distance to give them some privacy.

"Hey." He let his eyes travel down Jack's body, over the tux that fit him so perfectly well. "Hanging in there?" Jack had spent a few hours in the photo line.

"Doing better now." Jack winked and took a sip of his own champagne. "So." His eyes twinkled. "What's a gorgeous guy like you doing in a place like this?"

Ethan laughed, throwing his head back, as Jack kept smiling. "You trying to flirt with me, Mr. President?"

"Maybe."

"Mmm, I'm afraid I'm already taken, Mr. President."

"Is that so?" Jack's eyebrows shot straight up.

"By the most amazing man. He's absolutely perfect."

"Do tell me more about this great man." Jack's eyes glowed. "Will I have to have him taken out?" He stepped close enough that their sides brushed. "I'm the president, you know."

"Nothing could pull me away from him, Mr. President." It was a joke, their flirting, but Ethan's voice dropped, almost like he was vowing. He swallowed, and his eyes caught on the gazes fixed their way, and how half the room was staring at them and pretending not to. "He's got a smile that makes me weak in the knees."

Slowly, Jack smiled. "Oh yeah?"

Ethan's knees wobbled. "Oh yeah."

Their eyes met and held as Jack took a sip of his champagne, his Adam's apple rising and falling. Jack reached out, tracing one finger over the back of Ethan's hand. "I really want to dance with you," he whispered.

Ethan balked. He stared at Jack, his jaw dropping. That was not surreptitious. That was not staying out of the limelight. That was not being circumspect. That was nothing they had agreed on.

What would happen to Jack's presidency if they were more forward? If they stepped out into the spotlight? Senator Allen was already beating the drums against Jack for nothing more than their very secretive relationship and one public kiss on the White House lawn after the attempted coup. They were trying to salvage Jack's career, not sink it further.

"Jack… I thought—"

Jack stepped back. "You're right. Sorry." He shook his head. "I forgot it's not all about me. Your career matters, too. Rebuilding at the Secret Service." He took a quick sip of champagne and watched the band play.

"I don't care about that. It's your presidency that's more important. That asshole senator is here. I don't want to give him anything to use against you."

Jack's big blue eyes turned back to him. "Nothing is more important than us, Ethan. And no one can ever use you against me."

Ethan's heart stopped. "Jack—"

"I want to be *with* you," Jack whispered. "*Really* with you, Ethan. Like this isn't a scandal. I want you by my side in those photos I just had to take. I don't want you hanging out in the corners. I don't want you to be my dirty little secret."

He stared into Jack's eyes, filled with a mixture of love and aching sadness.

"I guess we do what we have to do, though," Jack whispered again. "Right?"

Ethan reached for Jack's champagne and set it and his own on the windowsill behind him. Jack froze when Ethan held out his hand. "May I have this dance, Mr. President?"

The brass band was playing a swing rendition of "Jingle Bells", and the dance floor was crowded. Guests, though, were paying attention to Jack and Ethan, and more gazes had turned their way.

Jack took Ethan's hand. "Are you sure?"

"I'm sure." Ethan led Jack to the dance floor. "But you're going to lead." He stopped, and a space seemed to clear for them. Jack's hand fell to his hip and Ethan gripped Jack's bicep. Their hands rose.

Jack stepped off, leading Ethan in a simple sway-and-swing as the band played on.

Cameras flashed, press photographers, cell phones, and personal cameras going wild. Jack beamed, though, staring into Ethan's eyes, and Ethan gazed back, transfixed by Jack's radiant joy. His cheeks ached; God, he was smiling wider than he ever had.

Eventually, the band wound down, transitioning to a slower song, a wailing jazz blues version of "Silent Night." Jack pulled Ethan close, tucking their heads together, and rested his hand on Ethan's back. Ethan mirrored him, cradling Jack's other hand against his chest, and they swayed as one, no space between them, moving together while the music carried them away. Jack's cheek pressed against his. Ethan closed his eyes.

More room opened up on the dance floor, a bubble surrounding them as the crowd watched. Ethan could feel their stares, could feel their questions, but he pushed it all away and nuzzled Jack's cheek.

A moment later, he felt Jack's lips press against his skin. Grinning, Ethan pulled back, gazing at Jack as the rest of the world faded away. Jack was smiling that wondrous smile of his, the one that made Ethan's heart beat faster and convinced him to break all his own rules. They gazed into each other's eyes as they kept dancing, their foreheads resting together, and traded soft kisses in between smiles and gentle giggles.

It was all over the front page of every newspaper the next morning.

Their dancing was newsworthy, apparently, crowding alongside reports of the military buildup in anticipation of the coming invasion against the Caliphate and the media's speculation of when it would occur. The trashier papers openly speculated about their relationship, calling the dance into question in light of the weeks and weeks of gossip about them being on the rocks and about to call it quits. More stately news organizations printed the photos and commented on the historicalness of the occurrence.

The best papers chose the photo that captured the light in Jack's eyes, his love and wonder and joy, and the bashful smile Ethan had, as if he couldn't hold his happiness in.

Scott had a copy of that photo—a front-page blowup that covered half the sheet—on his desk in Horsepower the next morning, Christmas Eve. Ethan spotted it when he walked in The agents there all clapped good-naturedly.

Scott rolled his eyes. "You gonna bother us all today?" He pulled Ethan into a quick hug, though, and tugged out a chair for him.

Jack was still the president on Christmas Eve and still had a day of work to take care of. He'd promised Ethan, over lingering kisses and an extreme reluctance to leave their bed, to be out of the West Wing by early afternoon. Ethan had laughed and shooed him away.

He had his own missions to take care of.

"Did you bring it?"

"Yeah, of course I brought it." Reaching behind him, Scott pulled a shopping bag from under his desk. "The guys at the scanners thought I was nuts."

Ethan grinned. He'd shipped his Christmas gifts for Jack to Scott and asked him to bring them to the White House so he could smuggle them in without Jack knowing. Scott had grumbled, but agreed.

Inside the bag, a teddy bear in a dark suit and tie sat next to a smaller box wrapped in navy satin and tied with a white bow. He pulled both out and set them on Scott's desk.

"Why the hell are you giving the president of the United States a teddy bear?" Scott's gruff voice tangled with his skeptical frown, and he glared at Ethan across his desk.

"Because." Ethan reached into his pocket and pulled out a package of white kids' shoelaces curled into a stiff spiral and a travel sewing kit. "It's going to be a Secret Service agent teddy bear." He grinned at his friend. "And he will love it. Do you have scissors?"

Scott groaned and tipped his head back, rubbing his hands over his face as a few agents standing around them laughed out loud at Ethan's foolishness. "You're ridiculous," Scott grunted, tossing a pair of scissors across his desk.

Standing, Scott shook his head at Ethan, but his eyes were bright. "I'm gonna do rounds. Don't burn down my White House, Salad Reichenbach."

"*Your* White House?" he scoffed. "It was mine before yours!"

"Yeah, yeah." The door slammed shut behind Scott, sealing Horsepower off from the White House. The rest of the agents within faded away from Ethan, back to their duties—watching monitors, manning radios, and interfacing with H Street and intel squads. The low hum of Horsepower continued around Ethan, and in the dim light of the bunker, he got to work.

A few cuts later, he had a spiral-curled spring of shoelace stretching from behind the teddy bear's ear to the collar of his dark suit. He stitched the shoelace into the bear's seams, tying the knots tight, and then sat it on the desk.

The bear was ridiculous, and totally cheesy, and he felt like a complete sap just sitting in front of the damn thing... but Jack would love it. It was a Secret Service bear.

Just like him.

"I hope that's not all you got him."

Ethan jumped. He glared at Scott, hovering over his shoulder. "No. His real gift is that." He jerked his chin to the blue satin box.

The satin was dark and the white bow just a decoration, curving around the lid. Scott reached for the slim box and flipped the hinged top. He whistled.

"There's a long history of first ladies giving presidents watches," Ethan grunted. He pressed his lips together, rubbing them back and forth. Shrugged. "Seemed like a good idea."

"Nice watch." Scott snapped the lid closed and set it—carefully—back on his desk. "You looking for an upgrade in your status?"

"Shut up. I didn't know what to do. I don't even know if he'll like it."

"He will." Scott reached into his suit jacket and pulled out a rolled-up white paper bag with the seal of the White House Gift Shop. "Got you something for your bear."

Ethan reached in and pulled out a pair of the toddler sunglasses the gift shop sold, the words "Secret Service Agent" etched in white on the arms. Something cute for little kids, and a brilliant idea for his gift. He slid the sunglasses over his teddy bear's glass eyes.

They just fit, and it completed the entire package. "Thanks."

Scott grunted.

"Hey." Ethan spun in his chair, squinting up at his friend. "There's something else I need your help with."

14

Scott pulled the blacked-out SUV into the middle deck of a parking garage down the street from the Hoover building, the FBI's DC headquarters. He stopped in the middle of a mostly empty aisle of cars.

Down the line, another black SUV flashed its headlights at Scott. "There they are."

Slowly, Scott rolled forward, pulling in beside the similarly blacked-out SUV.

"Be back in a few." Ethan hopped out the back door, sliding from the darkness of the SUV, and jumped into the front seat of the car they'd pulled up next to. He had a hoodie and sunglasses on, and kept his face downcast.

"Oh, fuck me," the driver of the second SUV growled when Ethan shut the passenger door behind him and pulled his hood down. "Collard said *he* wanted to meet. He didn't say anything about *your* dumb ass."

"It's your lucky day, Smithson." Ethan smirked at the FBI agent beside him. Special Agent Smithson was Scott's—once Ethan's—counterpart on the FBI's top-level intel squads run out of FBI headquarters. If there was a case of note happening in the United States, Smithson would be in the loop on it.

"What the fuck do you want, Reichenbach?" Smithson leaned away from him, into the driver's door, as if he could physically get farther away.

They'd always had a contentious relationship, but even this was extreme. Ethan glared. "Hey, fuck you too, all right? I'm only here because your guys in the Midwest iced me out of an investigation."

"Everyone who is smart is going to ice you out, Reichenbach. You're fucking kryptonite." He huffed, shifted again. "Say what you want and get the fuck out. I don't even want to chance anyone fucking seeing us together."

"There's a case in the Midwest region. Your guys have it locked down tight. You're chasing a woman with the alias 'Mother'—"

"Fuck," Smithson hissed. "You're *not* getting involved in that. Fuck you."

"I already *am* involved. Two dead girls linked to Mother have counterfeit bills shoved down their throats. Those bills are *my* investigation."

"And we'll send you the CliffsNotes version of our investigation when we're done. Cool your jets, turbo. You can't save your reputation by popping a couple of counterfeiters, you know. Or by edging into our turf."

"I don't want your turf, asshole. I want this thing done. And I've got something you don't have."

"Oh yeah? What's that? A ruined career? Bad fucking decisions, one after the other?"

Ethan ground his teeth. "I've got an asset who is an associate of Mother. Kid who was human trafficked. Knows the vics. Ran with Mother for a while. Let me in on the case. I can work this girl for you guys."

"Fuck," Smithson snapped. His fist hit the steering wheel and he shook his head, staring out the windshield as his face tightened. "You *had* to get involved in this fucking case, didn't you?"

"Did you know about the human trafficking?"

"We can't prove it." Smithson cursed again. "You have someone who was actually trafficked?"

"By another group. Her and others were 'rescued' by this Mother."

"It's all fucking connected out there, you know? There's a reason we don't want you anywhere near this shit. You could bring it all down. All of it."

Ethan stayed silent.

Smithson grabbed his keys, still in the ignition, and turned them hard. "I'll make a call. But know this, asshole. You're gonna be a ghost out there. You're nothing. You can't use this shit to make a new name for yourself." Smithson glared at Ethan as his lip curled.

"I'm bringing my partner, too."

"The fuck you are—"

"He'll be the face man. I'll be a ghost. Deal or no deal?"

"Fuck you, Reichenbach. Get the fuck out of my car."

"Text Collard when you want to actually play ball. Until then, fuck you too, Smithson." Ethan slid out of Smithson's SUV and slammed the passenger door so hard the SUV rocked back and forth. A second later, Smithson peeled out, the car's black plating brushing over the back of Ethan's hoodie.

He hopped into the back of Scott's SUV and blew out a hard exhale.

"Looked like that went well." Scott slid the vehicle into gear.

"I fucking hate Smithson. I am not sorry to be gone from his shit show."

"He's good with what he does. He and I haven't had a blowup yet. Not like you and him. Jesus, I think hating the FBI is your personal thing."

"They're pricks." Ethan leaned back, running his fingers through his hair. "Sorry if I fucked up your working relationship with him."

"He'll get over it." Scott pulled back into the DC traffic, navigating back to the White House. "Did you get what you needed?"

"Don't know yet. He kicked me out."

Scott grinned. "That's FBI-speak for you won. Congratulations."

Ethan snorted. He stared out the window until they made it back to the White House, and Scott parked them underground as if they'd never left.

Jack kept his word and left the Oval Office just after two in the afternoon, kicking out his staff when a slow snowstorm started falling over DC. He headed down to Horsepower and picked up Ethan, who'd been hanging out with the agents he used to serve with, playing a pickup game of Nerf basketball with the hoop suction-cupped to the mirrors in the back.

Jack good-naturedly played a round with the agents. They went easy on him, and Ethan watched as he perched on Daniels's desk, grinning.

They headed up to the Residence after, and Jack steered him toward the Study's closed doors. He hesitated, though, holding the doorknob and pressing his lips together.

"I hope this is okay."

Ethan kissed his hand, their fingers laced together. "It will be."

Jack blushed. He pushed the door open.

A squat Christmas tree, almost as tall as Ethan, stood next to the crackling fireplace. Simple decorations dotted the tree, baubles, colored balls and twinkling multicolored lights. Three wrapped packages sat beneath. On the mantel, evergreen boughs stretched across the white wood and two stockings hung from silver hangers shaped like snowflakes.

One stocking was embroidered with "Jack." The other, "Ethan."

The lights were low, and candles flickered on the tables in front of and beside the couch. Soft golden light suffused the study, already worn and warm and comfortable with old American furniture and portraits of American history hanging on the walls, next to the cranberry wallpaper and bronze sconces.

"I set everything up in here because I wanted to look at it while I was working in the evenings." Jack's hands disappeared into his pockets as he shrugged. "Wanted to think about it. You know. Our Christmas together."

Ethan pulled Jack close and pressed a kiss to his temple and then his lips before wrapping him up from behind and resting his chin on his shoulder. "It's perfect," he breathed. "Absolutely perfect."

Jack turned, draped his arms over Ethan's shoulders, and kissed him back slowly.

15

White House

Christmas morning dawned with DC blanketed in a winter wonderland.

Jack nuzzled Ethan under the heavy covers, his warm body sliding against Ethan as he slowly woke up. Jack's hands roamed over Ethan's body, his shoulders, his chest, down his arms, and around his stomach. Nuzzling turned to petting, and—when Ethan rolled over, pinning Jack to the mattress—petting turned to kisses and slow strokes, their bodies moving as one. They pressed together, from their toes to their endless kiss, rocking while Ethan laced their fingers and pressed their hands to the mattress next to Jack's head.

Jack's eyes blazed. He whimpered, shivering, and cried out when he came. Ethan followed, breathing in Jack's scent and kissing his hair before burying his face in Jack's neck.

"Merry first Christmas, love," Jack whispered into his ear.

Ethan pulled back. "First?"

"Our first together. More to come." He said it like it was a declaration, a promise, something Ethan could cling to and build a future on.

"Merry first Christmas, Jack."

Ethan made breakfast in his boxers while Jack sat and watched from the kitchen island, tangling his feet around Ethan's thighs every few minutes. When the cinnamon rolls were in the oven, Ethan pounced, lifting Jack from the island and carrying him to the couches in the West Sitting Hall. Laughing, Jack pulled Ethan down, and they made out while the snow tapered off outside the windows and the smell of warm cinnamon and fresh-squeezed orange juice filled the Residence.

They fed each other, Jack making a show out of licking the sticky mess off Ethan's fingers and giggling absurdly. Ethan swiped frosting on the tip of Jack's nose, over his chin, and along his neck, and then took far too long licking it off.

Jack's parents calling interrupted their antics. Jack answered with a hoarse voice, a little too raspy and a little too low, and Ethan flushed.

His mom and dad didn't mention it, though. Ethan traded his first nervous hellos with Jack's parents over speakerphone, Jack's warm eyes fixed on him, a soft smile permanently on his face.

"*Ethan?*" Jack's mother said. "*Is it really you? After all this time, we're finally talking?*"

"Yes, ma'am. It's me." He swallowed. "I'm sorry—"

"*It's all right; we're finally talking now. You two having a good Christmas so far?*"

"Yes, ma'am." He hoped his huge smile translated into his words, into his voice, for Jack's mom.

"*Well, I'm looking forward to meeting you, Ethan. Come down to Texas sometime. Bring my son, too.*"

Ethan laughed. "I will, ma'am. I'm looking forward to meeting you both as well."

"*We've got to meet the guy who has made our son this happy.*" A new voice broke in over the line, an older man. Ethan froze as Jack's head dipped, but he kept smiling, looking up at Ethan as he braced his elbows on his knees. "*Haven't seen him like this in years. Whatever you boys are doing up there, keep it up.*"

Ethan coughed. Jack laughed and reached for the phone. "Okay, Dad, thanks for embarrassing him."

"*What? I didn't say—*"

"So what are you both up to today?" Jack redirected the conversation and winked at Ethan, and they listened to Jack's parents talk about making their way to church and then dinner with a few friends later that day.

"*Next year,*" Jack's mother said, steel in her voice, "*we'll all be at the White House together. Right?*"

"Right." Jack elbowed Ethan, and a moment later, Ethan echoed him. "Right!"

Snorting, Jack shook his head. "All right, Mom, we'll let you go. We've got to get ready for stuff here."

"*Merry Christmas, dear. Merry Christmas, Ethan.*"

They wished Jack's parents well and hung up.

Jack turned to Ethan, suddenly serious and clutching his phone tight.

"Every year…" He hesitated. "Every year, I call Leslie's parents. I know it's been… *forever*. But I still do it. Is that okay with you?"

What could he say to that? Ethan's stomach flip-flopped, but he nodded. Of course Jack would keep in touch with his dead wife's parents, would keep that connection alive.

Jack laced his fingers through Ethan's as he dialed and held his hand through the call.

Leslie's parents asked about him. Over the phone, Ethan heard them tell Jack they were happy he'd found someone again, finally. Were happy he was happy.

When Jack hung up, he leaned into Ethan and kissed him softly.

They got ready after that, showering and shaving and dressing in khakis and sweaters. Ethan traded "Merry Christmas" texts with Scott, Daniels, and Inada, and a few other agents. Sent one to Becker, after thinking too hard about it.

At noon, they headed downstairs, hand in hand, and helped the White House caterer set up a Christmas lunch Jack had arranged for the staff. Ham and turkey, stuffing and cranberries, cornbread, sweet potatoes, and green beans stretched across the State Dining Room's grand table. Jack stacked plates and rolled napkins stuffed with silverware, and Ethan helped ferry the heavy dishes and trays of glassware.

Ethan brought down a stack of Christmas cards that Jack had signed for everyone on duty and laid them out. Inside each, Jack had slid a hefty gift card to DC's premier steakhouse.

As they finished prepping, the first of the Secret Service agents came through—younger agents Ethan had supervised before his bump up to command and then his transfer away. They grinned and shook his hand, but took a much more professional and sedate tone with the president. Daniels trailed behind the younger agents, and he and Ethan hugged and wished each other a merry Christmas.

"You took the day?"

Daniels nodded, standing beside Ethan and waiting for his agents to grab their food. "I'm a single guy and my family is all in Cali. I'm not going to fly back for just a day. Besides, I learned from someone else that a great leader takes the sacrifice." He bumped Ethan's shoulder.

Ethan said nothing. Daniels gripped his shoulder before he moved off, and Ethan watched him save two seats at the big table after he grabbed his food.

Watch Officers from the Situation Room showed up next, and then the stewards and White House staff. Ethan and Jack hung back until everyone had gotten their food, and then they dug in and sat down with Daniels, surrounded by everyone. Jack, naturally, dove into a dozen conversations.

Lunch went long, everyone reluctant to leave, and they ended up laughing over empty plates well into the afternoon. Duty called, though, Watch Officers wandering back to the Situation Room, Secret Service agents bleeding away, until Jack and Ethan were alone. They cleaned the room themselves, stacking plates and glasses and knives in bins for the kitchen and bunching up dirty tablecloths onto a cart in the corner.

Daniels poked his head back in when they were finished. Jack detoured to the Residence before they followed him down to the garage and slid into one of the blacked-out SUVs, bundled up in wool coats, scarves, and gloves. Daniels drove them south, through the empty streets of DC as Ethan and Jack held hands and watched the city slip by outside the windows.

Eventually, they pulled to a stop within Arlington National Cemetery, snow crunching beneath their tires. They were alone, the cemetery a still, silent place. Marble headstones poked above the white snowdrifts, and beyond, frail branches scratched the sky next to evergreen trees dusted with powder.

Ethan unfolded a map showing the newer section of burials, and Jack collected the bouquet of winter-white roses he'd placed in the SUV.

Daniels hung back after they walked to the section of new graves. "Levi." Ethan turned to his friend. "Come with us?"

Daniels nodded.

Together, they walked through the recent burials, finding the eleven Secret Service Agents who had died in Black Fox's attack on the White House. Jack placed a white rose in the snow at each of their headstones as Daniels and Ethan shared memories of the fallen agents, stories from on duty and off, jokes and memories and pranks they had all pulled on each other. Jack listened to every word, smiling and sad at the same time, his eyes bright with both joy and grief and lined with unshed tears.

Dusk had fallen by the time they finished. Daniels led them both to the SUV with his flashlight, holding out his hand to steady Jack over the slippery ice frozen across the pavement. They drove home in silence, Ethan holding Jack close and Daniels glancing at them in the rearview every few minutes.

Ethan gave Daniels another hug when they got back. Jack shook his hand, and Daniels disappeared back to Horsepower while they headed to the Residence.

Ethan detoured Jack, though, tugging him toward the East Room.

The dance floor from the Christmas Ball was still spread out, the decorations still up. He turned just the chandeliers on, dimming the lights, and pulled out his phone. A few taps, and then slow Christmas music started up.

Ethan rested the phone on the mantel as "Santa Baby" belted from the speaker. He held out his hand.

Jack laughed but took Ethan's hand and spun in his arms. "You lead this time," he whispered, cupping Ethan's cheek with one hand as Ethan held the other to his chest.

They danced alone in the ballroom as the songs rolled on.

Eventually, Jack led Ethan back up the Residence and to the Study. A fire was already going, and Ethan's packages had been added under the tree.

Jack grabbed all five and carried them to the couch. Grinning, he passed the first present to Ethan. It was small and light, and Ethan's heart skipped a beat as he ripped the paper.

An ornament sat in his hands. A silver frame, and inside, a picture of him and Jack in front of the tree in the East Room when Daniels had taken their picture. It was after the kiss, when Jack was laughing out loud, turned toward the camera, and Ethan was staring at Jack, grinning like a little boy. On the bottom of the frame, engraved in bold swirling strokes, it read, "Our First Christmas."

Jack was quiet as Ethan stared at the ornament.

"It's perfect," Ethan whispered.

Jack gently plucked it from his palm and went to the tree. He picked a high branch, dead center, and slipped the satin ribbon around a finger of evergreen. It bobbed and bounced, but the ornament stayed on. "Now it's perfect."

When he sat, Ethan passed Jack the bigger of his two boxes. He couldn't smother his grin at all.

Jack tore into the wrapping paper and then the box. He burst out laughing, his head tipping back against the couch, before he slid the teddy bear out. "Aww." He fingered the curled bit of shoelace going from the bear's ear to his suit and the engraved sunglasses hiding his eyes. "Is this my stand-in Secret Service bear when you're not here?" Jack's eyes twinkled.

"Something like that." Ethan's cheeks were on fire. "I thought it would make you smile."

"I love it." Jack tucked the bear against his side and leaned over for a kiss. "He's going to be well loved. Almost as much as you."

Ethan chuckled, and then Jack tossed him a squat, small box, wearing a wild smirk. Suspicious, Ethan tore into the paper carefully, and then flipped the lid on the plain cardboard box inside. He pulled out a coffee cup.

But not any coffee cup. Someone had taken a picture of Jack and turned his portrait into a rainbow of modern art. Jack, from his campaign posters, with his amazing smile, done in streaks of bright, brilliant rainbow.

"I found it online." Jack laughed, still holding the teddy bear against him. "I thought it would make *you* smile."

"This is amazing. I'm going to take this to the office. They won't know what to do."

"No one will steal your cup, that's for sure."

"Oh, God, no." Ethan set his new coffee cup on the table.

He hesitated. His smile faded. Chewing on the corner of his lip, he passed Jack his second and final gift. Had he gone too serious? Jack's gifts had been light and fun, but his next veered sharply from all that.

Jack turned to face Ethan, tucking one leg beneath him and plopping the bear in his lap as he picked apart the wrapping paper.

Ethan's lips thinned when Jack got to the dark blue satin. He couldn't look away.

Slowly, Jack lifted the lid and froze.

"Wow," he finally breathed, just when Ethan thought his heart was going to burst.

"This is a… *really* nice watch."

He'd gone all-out, getting something tasteful and classy, not boastful, but something he had to dip into his savings to afford. "I, uhh." Ethan cleared his throat. "I had the back engraved."

Jack's eyes darted to his before he plucked the watch from its satin pillow. Ethan watched him read the words Ethan had agonized over for days: *J, All of my hours and all of my minutes now belong to you. ~ E*

He held his breath, waiting.

"Ethan..."

"There's, uh, a long history of first ladies giving presidents watches. In the old days, pocket watches. And then wristwatches." He scratched the back of his neck, trying to hide his grimace as Jack stayed silent. "I just thought it would be, you know, a historical touch." Silence. Ethan wanted to disappear.

Jack held out the watch in one hand and turned his other wrist over. "Will you put it on me?" His eyes were burning, his gaze brimming with joy—with love—and he had one of the biggest smiles on his face that Ethan had ever seen.

His fingers shook as he wrapped the leather band around Jack's wrist, and his gaze lingered on his engraving right before the words pressed against Jack's skin. It felt bigger than just a watch, bigger than just a Christmas present, and he kissed the inside of Jack's wrist above the clasp after he finished.

Jack reached for him, tugged him close, and kissed him soft and sweet. "I love it," Jack whispered against his lips. "I love *everything* about it. Thank you."

Smiling, Ethan pressed his forehead to Jack's and closed his eyes.

"You have one more gift."

He reached for Jack's last present. It was slim and flat, and as Ethan tore into the paper, it was Jack's turn to bite his lip. Jack gripped his new bear, his eyes wide. The wrapping paper fell to the carpet.

A book sat in Ethan's hands, hardbound in navy blue. Printed on the cover, beneath the same picture of him and Jack from the Rose Garden that he had tucked away on his desk in Des Moines, were the words "Year One."

He breathed in slowly, flipping the book open.

Pictures from the campaign dotted the first half page, followed by Jack's election victory night. In every picture, Jack was there, but so was Ethan. Him, in the corner of the frame, serious and glowering over the crowd. Him, protecting Jack on a handshake line. He turned the page. Jack, just before the Inauguration Parade, and him at his side.

"I asked Pete to pull every photo of the two of us. Even ones before we were together." Jack shrugged, and his fingers played with his bear's tie, plucking at the fabric. Photos of him and Jack at Camp David, laughing side by side, captured by the White House photographer. Images back in DC, him holding the door for Jack as he entered the Oval Office. They were both smiling, and there was something there, something in their gazes that stole Ethan's breath. Even before everything, even before they were secretly hanging out—not even dating, not even friends— there was raw electricity crackling between them.

Pictures of him hanging out in the Oval Office, chatting with Jack. Before The Kiss, but after he'd given Jack his cell phone number. When they were... not dating, but more than colleagues.

Him and Jack, walking back to the Residence at the end of the day, the Rose Garden on their right in brilliant bloom. Jack, his jacket off and thrown over one shoulder, laughing at something Ethan had said. Ethan, shaking his head and looking down, supposedly escorting Jack and *not* planning on sneaking up to meet him in the Residence shortly after.

Prague. His fingers stuttered on the page. Between the last picture and Prague, his foolish kiss had happened beside the pool table in the game room.

There was a picture of him at Jack's side, climbing out of the presidential SUV right before he met with Puchkov for that fateful early morning meeting. Jack had leaned into his side, and Ethan had wanted to grab him and hold on forever. Jack's face was tight and Ethan looked ready to brawl, but they were angled toward each other, almost desperately, as if they wanted to turn toward the other and knelt into his arms. He had felt *exactly* like that, but he thought he'd done a better job hiding it.

Another image, him shadowing Jack making the rounds at the cocktail reception after. His eyes were fixed on Jack as Jack spoke with the German chancellor.

And then, the next page, when Air Force One landed stateside after Prague. Someone had captured a picture of Jack passing him his jacket that he'd left in Jack's cabin on Air Force One, and the way they were beaming at each other—

Well. It was no wonder Scott had figured it all out that moment.

Pages of pictures after, mostly official ones from the White House photographer. Apparently they had been a favorite subject of his. No guessing why. There was something in each photo of the two of them. Something special. Something electric. Something hidden and raw, like there were secrets in the depths of their eyes, in the touch of their hands. Of course, there *were*. In one photo, Ethan escorted Jack down the West Wing hallway, his hand ghosting over the small of Jack's back.

"I shouldn't have done that."

"I always loved it when you did."

More pictures of the two of them drinking coffee in the White House mess. Jack perched on the Resolute desk, listening to Ethan outline a security plan for one of their trips. The two of them in the Rose Garden, passing a football back and forth as Scott and Daniels watched, bemused. Them, looking into each other's eyes as Jack passed by Ethan, walking into the Oval Office and so close they were almost touching. Walking side by side down the Cross Hall, a little too near for propriety's sake.

Selfies from Jack, the first of many. Them on the Truman Balcony. Them side by side on the couch. Jack laughing next to a blushing Ethan, standing in just his boxers and holding his pool stick. A picture Ethan had never seen, him asleep against Jack's shoulder on the couch and Jack pressing a kiss to his hair as he looked at the camera.

Ethan's cheeks ached, and he took a shaky breath. "This is…"

"Keep going."

He turned the page.

Jack accepting his folded flag in Arlington, looking like his world had ended.

Jack, one hand hovering over Ethan's coffin.

Jack, sobbing, nearly collapsing into the coffin, barely able to stand.

"I didn't know if I should leave those. But they happened. They're part of us."

It took a few swallows, but Ethan finally managed to get past the lump in his throat. His fingers traced over Jack's bowed back, the despair in his face.

He turned the page.

A printout of the news headline and a picture of Jack on the day he told the world that he and Ethan were more than friends, more than colleagues. That he *loved* Ethan.

"I'm so sorry," Ethan murmured. "That you had to do that—"

"I didn't have to. Pete told me to deny it. I *chose* to say what I said."

"Why?" Ethan frowned, and he finally turned away from the photos. "*Why*, Jack? Why did you reveal it all? You could have avoided all of this—"

"Because I loved you, and I still do love you. You deserved more than to be forgotten or ignored. I thought you were gone, and I wanted to do the right thing for your memory."

"I'm so sorry."

"I'm sorry I did it without you." Jack's expression twisted, frustration and guilt at war with each other. "When you did come back... I'd changed your entire world. You didn't even get a choice about it." He plucked at the bear again. "I feel bad about that."

His eyes opened and caught on their Christmas tree. On their matching stockings. Wandered back to their ornament and the picture within the small frame. Would they have had any of this if they hadn't been outed? If they had to stay in hiding?

He reached for Jack's hand. "I told you before. I wouldn't change anything. This, all of this, is exactly what I want."

Jack smiled, squeezing Ethan's hand. "There's more." He pointed back to the book.

Ethan turned to the next page.

One photo, blown up to cover both pages. Him kissing Jack in the back of the ambulance on the White House North Lawn after everything had gone down. After Black Fox, and Jeff, and Ethan helping Jack out of the destroyed White House.

"'The kiss that shook the world'." Jack shook his head, but he smiled.

The rest of the pages were a mix of pictures from Jack's phone and the media. The two of them together in the White House, walking with Ethan's arm around Jack's waist, Jack's arm in a sling. Jack presenting Daniels, Welby, Inada, and Scott with medals, and Ethan hanging back, clapping for his friends. Jack taking a selfie of them both, their matching black eyes fading away. A selfie taken while they were kissing, and another one where Jack's gaze had wandered to the camera mid-kiss, but the pure love in his blue eyes stopped any protest Ethan might have made.

Screenshots of Ethan over Skype, smiling, blushing, laughing.

Shots from the weekends. Drinking beers together. A selfie watching the Super Bowl. Another official photo, this time from behind, the two of them in silhouette with their hands clasped, standing on the Truman Balcony and gazing at the Washington Monument.

Jack's selfies from the Christmas tour and the pictures Daniels had taken. Even the one Daniels had sneaked in, the group selfie of the agents grinning for Jack's camera.

Finally, on the last page, pictures from the Christmas Ball only days before. Him and Jack dancing and gazing into each other's eyes, smiling and sneaking kisses. Christmas trees and golden decorations floated in the background, but Jack's smile and the love in Ethan's eyes stole the soul of the picture.

"We did everything in-house. Turns out, you can get things pretty quickly around here if you're the president." Jack leaned into Ethan's shoulder, smiling.

"This is…" He didn't know what to say. Amazing? Unbelievable? Perfect? He shook his head. "It's—" How did he quantify this gift, a seemingly simple book of pictures with the one man who made his soul feel like it was on fire? God, it was so much more than just a Christmas present. It was almost like a declaration. "Year One," implying more years. Permanence. It was printed. It was bound. There was no shoving this away, no hiding what it was. Their love, their life. Here to stay. How did he react to everything swirling in his heart and his head, unlocked by the gift Jack had given him?

"*Us.*" Jack pressed a kiss to his shoulder. "It's us." Another kiss, and Jack's cheek rested on the curve of his shoulder. "I love you."

He finally found some words but still fumbled, as if speaking was something brand-new to him, some trick of a more evolved creature. "This is," he started slowly, "the single best gift I have ever received." Ethan turned to Jack and cradled his face in both hands. "I love you," he breathed, "more than I can ever say."

Jack's eyes closed as he smiled and leaned forward, nuzzling his forehead against Ethan's. After a moment, Ethan pulled Jack closer, lying back and tugging Jack until he was lying on top of him, the teddy bear mashed between the couch and their sides. Jack rested his cheek on Ethan's shoulder as Ethan stroked up and down Jack's back, watching the Christmas tree lights twinkle as he held the love of his life in his arms.

16

They stayed in bed almost all day on Saturday.

Ethan woke first, teasing Jack awake with a sloppy blowjob, until Jack's fingers gripped his hair and tugged as he came. He reciprocated, Ethan ripping Jack's bedsheets free from the corners of the mattress.

Later, Ethan grabbed his new coffee cup for them to share, bringing it back to bed along with the teddy bear and the photobook. They went through each page, every photo, reminiscing about their building friendship and their secretive relationship, and when they had to hide that they were dating while still working in the West Wing.

Clearly, in hindsight, they had done a piss-poor job hiding everything. It was all there in the way they looked at each other. How they stood a little too close. Ethan's hands lingering on Jack's back or his shoulder, or their smiles and gazes hanging for just a bit too long. Captured forever in official White House photos.

Jack's playful selfies of them both made Ethan's heart want to burst. Moments he remembered. Moments when Jack had taken a picture without him knowing.

Even though they wanted to ignore the world, and have the world ignore them for just one day, Jack was still the president and there was still an invasion only days away. Jack took phone calls, totally naked in bed, while Ethan slipped into the bathroom. He came back and nuzzled Jack's hip, kissed his belly, and laid his head on Jack's thigh. Jack's eyes blazed, burning as his fingers ran through Ethan's hair as he talked through the day's updates from his Joint Chiefs over the phone.

Ethan was too lazy to cook and Jack didn't want to disrupt the White House staff, so Ethan texted Daniels for the number of the pizza place they always ordered from down in Horsepower. Forty-five minutes later, Daniels texted back that their pizza was coming up the elevator.

They moved to the Study to eat and watch a movie, curled up together by the light of the tree. The sun set, but they kept the lights off, aside from the decorations.

After the movie ended, Jack started a fire and spread a blanket on the floor before the flames, pulling throw pillows down with him. He tried to hide setting their bottle of lube and a condom near the tree, within reach but tucked away. Burnished light played over his skin, over his bare chest, and teased at the waistband of his boxers.

"C'mere," Jack breathed, holding his hand out to Ethan when he was done. His eyes lingered on Ethan's body, trailed over his chest and his legs.

Ethan went, smiling as he landed beside Jack. Heat from the fire tickled his arms, the backs of his knees.

They kissed slowly as the fire warmed their bodies, prickled sweat against their skin. One of Jack's hands cupped Ethan's cheek and Ethan's heart fluttered. "I want to suck you," Jack murmured against his lips. "Is that okay?"

He moaned. "Yeah. 'Course."

Ethan lay back, propped on his elbows with his legs spread as Jack crawled between them. Jack reached for the lube, set it beside Ethan's thigh, and wiggled a throw pillow beneath Ethan's hips. And then—

Ethan tipped his head back, groaning and cursing. Jack's mouth was hot, his moves slow and just sloppy enough to be almost scandalous. Salacious, even. His was the only cock Jack had ever sucked, and that made his soul shiver.

He'd thought Jack blowing him would be a rare occurrence. Would be something that maybe he'd miss, but he would do without for his love of Jack.

He'd long lost count of how many times Jack had sucked him, swallowed him whole.

God, Jack sucked him with that perfect combination of hot and sweet, sloppy and tender. Like it was his first time, every single time.

Or like he really, truly enjoyed it, enjoyed making Ethan's thighs clench and quiver.

His legs trembled, lines of fire racing through him. How was he this lucky? How was this his life?

And then, Jack's finger, already slick, slid past his balls.

God, yes. Ethan lifted his leg, resting his foot gently on Jack's shoulder. His toes curled, and then his foot, and he barely held back the quiver that jolted through him when Jack's finger rubbed over his hole. He was warm, dizzy from too many sensations: the heat of the fire and the suction of Jack's mouth, the press of Jack's fingers against his entrance. The stretch. The thought of Jack, opening his body up—

Jack had learned enough to know how to stretch and loosen, when to wait, and when to stroke. Ethan whimpered and fell back when Jack pressed his fingers deep, just behind his cock.

With Jack, everything was like raw lightning. Or a forest fire, scorching heat moving in forceful waves through him. His body was blazing, making him shiver, and a part of him felt slick and messy and open, craving in a way that was almost primal. Needy. Jack was inside him, in a place where no other had been, and though he'd thought it would be invasive, would be something that spread him open too much, he almost couldn't believe it when he wanted more. Each and every time, more and more of Jack.

Jack sat back and wiped his arm across his face, smearing his spit as one shaking hand reached for the condom. He tore it with his teeth, and Ethan watched it all. Watched Jack's shoulders heave as he breathed hard and fast. Watched the flush of his chest, crimson in the firelight. Watched him spit out the wrapper and bite his lip as he worked the condom down his cock and fumbled for the lube. More lube slicked against his ass, and he saw Jack squirt some on himself, shivering as he stroked it over his condom-covered cock before wiping his slick fingers over Ethan's thigh, up to the back of his knee. Lube smeared on his skin, but Ethan didn't care.

Ethan's mouth hung open, panting as he waited. Jack moved closer, lining them up, his tongue poking out as he pressed the blunt head of his cock against Ethan's opening. He bit his lip and pushed.

Ethan grasped Jack's arms, his breath leaving him, all his oxygen replaced by the feel of Jack entering him. The ache, the heat, the craving. He pulled his legs farther apart. The stretch, the feeling of being breached. Of Jack filling him, and his body opening for Jack's cock.

Gasping, Jack sank all the way in. He paused, hovering over Ethan as their bodies locked together, joined as close as two men could possibly be. Ethan's cock rose between them, swollen and dark. Jack stared down, smiling like he was looking at something breathtakingly beautiful.

"So gorgeous," Jack whispered. "Ethan, you're so gorgeous."

Ethan swallowed. His hands fluttered down Jack's arms, skipping over his skin. Rounded his elbows, his thumbs stroking over his biceps. Jack was sleek where Ethan was not, tanned skin soft and smooth unlike Ethan's coarser skin, his scars, and his hair. "I'm not—" He grunted, his body still welcoming Jack within. "I'm not too…" How did he finish that thought? His words were fleeing him, his thoughts reduced to base desires and needs and fears. "Male?"

Confusion tangled in Jack's gaze for a moment. He blinked, and then it vanished, replaced by a hint of shock and then warm love. He leaned down, one hand stroking through Ethan's hair as he bent Ethan in half, keeping them joined. "You're *wonderfully* male," he said, his voice rough-edged, too deep. "I could never confuse you for anything else, Ethan. You're the *man* I fell in love with."

And then he started to move.

Ethan gritted his teeth and stared up at Jack. Jack moved slowly, rocking thrusts turning into long, deep slides in and out. Ethan shivered and writhed until Jack pulled his legs over his own arms, opening Ethan up completely. Jack had his whole body, his whole soul, in his grasp, and moved reverently, as if worshipping Ethan.

They'd done it all. Made love slow, sensual, and languid, kissing until their orgasms almost surprised them. Hard and fast—the furious reconnection of a week or more apart. But, in front of the fire, something new was building inside Ethan. Desire sizzled, coiling in his soul, so tight and clenched that he felt he would snap.

Jack kept a rolling pace, indolent in front of the fire, watching Ethan like he was trying to memorize him. Ethan's gasps and moans, the breathless way Jack's name fell from his lips... Jack's eyes caught it all, and Ethan burned beneath the intensity of his stare. He was turned entirely inside out by it.

Shifting, Jack bent Ethan a little bit more, enough so that they could tangle their lips together. Jack smiled down at him, eyes holding Ethan's gaze, as he snapped his hips into Ethan, deeper than before. Faster. Until he had a rhythm going, until Ethan was panting, openmouthed and staring up at Jack as he trembled, his hands clenching around Jack's shoulders. He hung on, rocking on Jack's thrusts, held entirely in Jack's embrace.

He got one hand on his cock, and Jack cursed, almost faltering. His eyes blazed. "Love seeing you touch yourself," Jack said, blushing as if it was an admission. "Love seeing you come. Seeing you fall apart."

"Fuck..." There was too much heat building everywhere, spreading through his body, and he was gasping against it, against the pressure. It all sharpened on one ragged inhale, and the world froze on Jack's next thrust. Ethan's body shattered, his orgasm tearing through him. He shouted, wordless cries and Jack's name as he shivered and shook and white-hot pleasure spiraled through him.

Jack whimpered, thrusting against Ethan, kissing him as much as he could around Ethan's pants and gasps, sucking on his lip, his chin. He faltered, moaning through clenched teeth, his shoulders heaving as his hips snapped against Ethan. He buried his cock as deep as it could go, all of him twitching and pulsing as he tried to breathe against the skin of Ethan's neck.

Ethan didn't want to let go. He held on, legs tangled in Jack's arms, desperately trying to wrap around his waist, his shoulder, anything he could reach. His hands slid through Jack's hair, fingers playing in the dirty-blond strands. They were still connected, still pressed so close, as if they could climb inside each other's skin and share one soul.

Eventually, Jack pulled back, and they lay on their sides facing each other, kissing slowly as the fire died, fingers tracing patterns into the skin of their shoulders, cheeks, and chests.

"All right," Jack hissed the next morning. He propped himself up on his elbows, peering down at Ethan on their bed. "I think I'm sexed out."

"Oh, thank God." Ethan exhaled, still shaking from their morning fumble and their latest orgasms. "That last one stung."

"I think I'm completely dry." Chuckling, Jack tucked his face into Ethan's neck, pressing a warm kiss to his skin. "He's retreating. White flag is up."

Ethan laughed, and his hands stroked up and down Jack's back, slow and gentle. "Was afraid I couldn't keep up with you."

Jack snorted. "I'll need all week to recover."

And then the light moment fled.

It was Sunday. And Ethan was leaving.

Ethan wrapped his arms around Jack, holding him close enough to feel Jack's rough swallow through their pressed chests.

"Five days," Jack breathed.

Ethan didn't know if he was talking about the time they'd just had, or the days between now and their next visit. Either way, it was a terrible number. Not long enough and far too long, all at the same time. "We still have the morning."

Except, not quite.

Jack was still the president and the phone rang even on Sundays. He fielded calls from Irwin and a longer one from the Joint Chiefs as Ethan made a feast for breakfast. French toast, eggs and bacon, orange juice and sliced fruit. Jack ate bites in between his morning brief, held on speakerphone in the kitchen, as Ethan stayed silent. He watched the play of Jack's hair in the winter sunlight, the curves of his shoulders beneath his T-shirt. The plump bow of his lips. Tried to burn it all into his memory and the backs of his eyelids.

By the time they were alone again, it was nearly time to pack. Ethan kept pushing it off, lingering by Jack's side in the kitchen as they flirted over coffee and traded smiles and jokes.

Until there was no time left at all, and he hurried through his shower as Jack threw his clothes, coffee mug, and photobook into his duffel, and Scott kept texting him to hurry up or he'd miss his flight. Jack had on jeans and his long overcoat, and Ethan couldn't remember what he threw on.

He had to leave earlier than usual. Jack had to get back to work. There was an invasion to manage and a war to win.

He kissed Jack in the elevator going down, holding him tight as his stomach fell further than the three floors they dropped. His tongue grew heavy and hard, thick with sorrow and frustration, and he didn't know what to say.

But Jack climbed into the SUV with him, holding his hand, and Ethan leaned his head against Jack's, grateful for the extra twenty-eight minutes they could share. The partition was up again, Scott and his driver giving them privacy for their last moments.

"It's on the twenty-ninth," Jack whispered. His fingers laced through Ethan's. "The invasion. It starts Tuesday. Airborne troops will drop into Iraq and Syria from Turkey and Jordan late Tuesday night. Russian troops are coming in from Georgia and Azerbaijan."

Ethan pressed a kiss to Jack's hair and held him close, inhaling his scent. "You're doing the right thing."

Silence as they rumbled through the streets of DC and turned onto the highway toward the airport.

At the turnoff to Dulles, Jack pulled back and reached into his coat. "I brought someone to drive back with me." He pulled out the teddy bear.

Ethan poked the bear's curled earpiece. "Watch over him, okay?" He spoke to the bear. "He's special. And you have a very special duty, protecting him while I'm gone."

Jack smiled, and then the SUV slowed down. Travelers milled outside the terminal, people lugging suitcases and hugging their loved ones goodbye. Reporters mingled at the entrance, photographers and cameramen who waited all day on Sundays just to be the first there, the one with the scoop, when Ethan arrived.

They perked up at the blacked-out SUV rolling to the curb.

The partition dropped. Scott looked back, grimacing. "I've got to stay with the president, Ethan. We've got chaser cars, but we're running a low profile. So say your goodbyes and slip out quick."

Ethan nodded. Jack's hand touched his cheek.

He could say "I love you" a thousand times to Jack and it would never be enough. Not in a lifetime, and not in the next minute. He saw the same frustration in Jack's eyes, the same pain, and instead of speaking, they pressed their foreheads together. "I'll see you soon, love," Jack breathed.

Ethan couldn't speak. He nodded and kissed Jack's cheeks, his closed eyelids, and then his lips, lingering until the sob building in his chest threatened to burst free. Grabbing his duffel, Ethan shoved open the car door and jumped out, shutting it behind him before anyone could see inside.

One step and then another. Photographers surrounded him. Hounded him. Cameras flashed and microphones shoved in his face. Questions shouted over each other, a racket of noise that almost had him disoriented.

"Ethan!"

Through it all, he heard his name perfectly, shouted from the one voice he wanted to hear more than any other. Whipping around, he spotted Jack pushing out of the SUV, and Scott, wide-eyed and pissed, tearing from the passenger side, trying to catch up. Cars crammed around Jack's SUV emptied, undercover agents running to catch and surround Jack. None of that mattered.

Jack was running toward *him*.

Ethan dropped his duffel and met Jack halfway, his arms wrapping Jack up, enveloping him as Jack's hands rose and cradled his face. A stuttered breath, their eyes meeting, and then they kissed, pressed as close together as two people could be. The kiss went down to his soul, and then further, something cosmic in the moment, something that reset orbits and stole the power of the sun.

Once, Ethan had seen a movie that spoke about four great kisses in the history of the world. *Step aside*, he thought. *This is the kiss of the ages.*

Jack's fingers were warm on Ethan's cheeks. Ethan's hands wound their way around Jack, up around his shoulders until he had one buried in Jack's hair. They were still kissing, even as the cameras flashed and the media caught it all in close-up, in screaming Technicolor, and Secret Service agents shouted for the crowds to get back. Passersby whipped out their cell phones, recording the entire tableau. It was all going live to the internet, Ethan was certain.

They finally parted. Ethan was unsteady, dizzy, and he clung to Jack, trying to find his balance. Jack was no better, holding on to the lapels of Ethan's coat, breathless and wide-eyed.

"Mr. President!" A reporter shouted. "Can you comment on the state of your relationship with Mr. Reichenbach?"

"What's it like to be separated, Mr. President? Having to say goodbye?"

Jack smiled. "I love you, Ethan," he said, ignoring the reporters held back by the scowling Secret Service agents surrounding them both.

"Hope so, after that." Ethan grinned as Jack laughed, throwing his head back. He kissed Jack's chin, and then Jack met his gaze again. "I love you, Jack."

"See you soon." Jack stepped back, a single step, and Scott and the others closed around him, whisking him away from Ethan and back to the SUV, surrounding him in their bubble of dark suits and fierce glares. Ethan watched them go, listened to the car doors slam the spin of tires against slush and cold concrete as Scott peeled away from the curb.

The media was still there, pressing in on him again, but Ethan grabbed his duffel and pushed through, the feel of Jack's lips still ghosting over his.

17

Jack plucked at his bear during the car ride back, trying to keep it together in front of Scott and his driver. There was a hole opening up in his chest, a dark, tangled mess of aching loss and grief. It was wrong to drive away and leave Ethan heading to Iowa. Wrong for them to be apart, when being together as they had been was so perfect.

Three years until he was out of office had once seemed like a short blip of time. It stretched before him now, a long string of stolen weekends and not nearly enough Ethan.

The partition hissed, lowering. Scott turned in his seat, looking back at Jack. He smiled at the bear. "He made that himself, you know. Sewed on the wire down in Horsepower."

Jack smiled, but it fractured as his fingers traced the stiff white curl from the bear's ear to his collar and back. "It's perfect." The watch Ethan had also given him pressed against his skin, almost too warm, like the engraved words were a promise against his soul.

"It sucks," Scott grunted. "Him being transferred. Having to go."

"It was better than being fired."

"Maybe. I dunno." Sighing, Scott shook his head. "Would have been cleaner if he was fired. This sucks."

He managed a sad smile as he played with the bear, waving his arms up and down. "Yeah."

Silence.

"We all miss him, too."

Jack finally looked up, meeting Scott's haggard gaze. He wasn't alone, not really. Not when he had Ethan's friends around him and their memories to sustain him. He spun the bear, waving one paw toward Scott. "Five days," he said, trying to grin when Scott snorted. "Five days until he's back."

Was there ever a way Ethan could stay? Could actually be by his side? Was there ever a chance he and Ethan could live like a normal couple… together? Albeit, in the White House? There was an unspoken question hovering around their relationship from nearly everyone in the media. Would Ethan eventually become his first gentleman? Could the White House—and the nation—accept a first gentleman? Was it even legal, or practical?

Would Ethan want that, if it were possible?

Maybe he'd look into it. Ask a few questions. Diana Ramirez, his counsel, was as good they came. If she knew of any legal basis for them to be together—officially, *really* together, living in the White House, the acknowledged first couple and everything else—then maybe there was a chance.

Maybe one day. If Ethan wanted.

18

Des Moines

"Jesus Christ, these reporters are everywhere."

"Yeah, I know." Ethan shouldered his duffel and glowered, trying to barrel through the crowd of photographers surrounding him. The curb and Becker's waiting car were just ahead. Becker sat in the front seat, glaring daggers at the press circling his car and turning their cameras on him.

Becker flashed his red and blues and laid on his horn. The photographers snapped more photos.

Finally, Ethan pushed through the crowd and slid into Becker's car. He slammed the door behind him, shutting off the shouted questions and the whirrs and clicks of the cameras. "Drive. Get us out of here."

There were media vans and photographer cars just waiting to tail them out of the airport. They'd get away, but not by much. Becker cursed, scowling as he veered right and left and tried to shake the reporters hounding them. Eventually, he lost them at a red light before driving onto the highway and heading for downtown.

"So," he said, giving Ethan the once-over. "How was it?"

Ethan shrugged. "Good." He wasn't about to say that it had been the best Christmas he'd ever had and possibly the single best extended weekend with Jack ever. Their kiss at the airport replayed near constantly in the back of his mind, an endless loop of Jack's voice calling his name, Jack's hands on his face, the way Jack's lips had tasted. How they had felt and how they seemed to speak straight to Ethan's heart and soul.

"Saw the news." Becker grinned. "Seemed like it went well."

"So we're not breaking up anymore?"

"Full-on reconciliation. Guess the guy is going to keep you." Becker winked as Ethan snorted.

"What about you?" Ethan hadn't heard from Becker once over the long weekend. "Good holiday?"

"Yeah." Shifting, Becker tried not to fidget but failed completely. One finger tapped over the steering wheel.

Ethan waited.

"Ellie worked Christmas day, so I met up with her. We had a cop's Christmas dinner with some of her patrol. You know, everyone crowded in a diner, eating crappy food." He tried but failed to hold back his smile. "It was awesome."

"Ellie, huh?" Ethan chuckled. The young lady friend Becker had made on the local police force. "What happened to her being out of your league?"

More fidgeting. A blush across Becker's cheekbones. "She asked me, actually."

"She got tired of waiting for you. I like it."

"Maybe we could all meet up some day. Get drinks. Or something." Shrugging, Becker jerked the car off the highway and down the exit ramp, taking them to the Federal Building and Ethan's car.

He kept quiet, letting Becker's comment hang. Could he be a normal person again? Would it be responsible to try? Between Jack, his presidency, and the limelight Ethan was constantly in, would bringing anyone else into the swirling insanity his world had become be even remotely a wise decision?

Or had his life irrevocably changed, and he had to make his peace with that, like Jack had had to make his peace with his new life when he stepped foot into the Oval Office?

"So, you said you'd have some stuff about our case when you got back." Becker changed the subject, speaking about their case only when he turned in to the underground garage, safely out of sight of the chasing media. "I hope you do, because another body was found yesterday. Another murdered girl. More bills stuffed in her mouth. You have anything for us to move forward with? Work on getting rid of this killer for good?"

"Fuck." Ethan cursed, sighing heavily as the news of the third murdered girl sank in. "I do. Actually, I have a lot." Scott had texted him late Saturday, relaying a message from Smithson: an address in Des Moines on the other side of the city from the Federal Building, and a time on Monday morning. "We're joining the FBI task force working the Mother case."

Becker whipped around in his seat. "What?"

"I told them we had access to a key witness and we could work with her until she converted to working with them. We've got to get back to Gabriela. Get her to give us a little more on Mother."

"How are we going to do that? You saw her last time."

"I did. I saw how much those girls' deaths affected her. I'm betting this girl is also connected, and Gabriela will be just as upset. She's got to make a choice. Does she help us find Mother? Hopefully help find this killer? Put an end to her friends' deaths? Or not?"

Becker whistled. "Jesus, I do not envy her. Not when you go and lay it on like that. That's a shitty choice you're giving her."

"Not me. Life." Ethan shoved open the door. His muscles were taut, like he had to run, had to burn something off. Frustration, perhaps. The anger of having left Jack and coming back to find another young woman murdered. The case wasn't theirs—they weren't the ones who were supposed to be working the murders, weren't the ones who were supposed to be finding Mother. They were financial crimes. They caught counterfeiters. Not murderers.

But like everything else in Ethan's life, the lines had become blurred. He was pursuing something he had no business getting involved in, but he couldn't let it go. And the choices he—and everyone else—had were fantastically shitty. What was the right choice? What would be best? Where was the clear path, the one leading to the happy ending?

"We meet at the jail tomorrow morning. Before dawn. Before we head over to the FBI's secure site."

Becker nodded.

Ethan grabbed his duffel and climbed out of Becker's car, fishing his keys out of his pocket and unlocking his own with the remote. "Thanks for—" He shrugged, gesturing to the car, the ramp, and the media outside. Becker had volunteered to dive into his craziness, and he didn't need to.

Becker tried to smile, but it was thin. "No problem, man. See you tomorrow."

It was as awful as he expected it to be. Perhaps even worse.

They met at the jail just after four in the morning. Ethan had too many jitters and too much coffee in his veins, helped by a nice dose of adrenaline. Becker didn't say much, but he brought breakfast for them.

They broke the news of the third murder better than the last time. She was most likely an associate, even a friend, of Gabriela's, and Ethan prepped Gabriela as best he could before delivering the message. She sobbed, and they let her, passing over tissue after tissue.

Ethan held his hand out across the table while she was gulping down her tears, swallowing air in big hiccups as she hugged herself tight. She hesitated, but then reached for his hand, holding on until her knuckles went white. He waited until her breathing leveled out and she sat up straight. Looked him in the eyes and tried to smile, a watery thank-you.

Gabriela told them all about the murdered girl, still a Jane Doe in the county morgue. Who she was and how she knew her. How they'd come across the border together and started working the streets for their coyote. And then—

Her mouth closed with a snap when she got to the part where she'd been rescued. When she got to Mother.

"Gabriela, I know what it's like." Ethan shifted, crossing his legs as he bit the inside of his lip. "To have to make the best of a bad decision. When everything seems like it's only going to get worse."

She watched him, her wary eyes bright with unshed tears.

"I know what it feels like when you'd rather die than hurt the ones you love. But I am asking you. *Please*. Help us find Mother. We need to talk to her. Find out why these girls, these girls all connected to her, have been found dead." Gabriela looked away. Her chin quivered.

"She's done bad things," Gabriela breathed. "Not just good."

"Haven't we all?"

"You'll arrest her." Tears cascaded down Gabriela's cheeks. "She's my savior. She saved me. She answered my prayers. How can I just turn on her like that?"

He held out his hand again, stretching it across the table toward her. "Help us stop the next murder. Please."

Gabriela's fingers inched across the cold steel table.

She gripped his hand and started to speak.

In the FBI's secure site dedicated to the investigation, Becker and Ethan were led to a conference room and dumped for over an hour.

Becker almost blew his lid.

"You know what to do?" Ethan asked softly when they finally heard voices outside their door.

A single nod was all he got in response.

Grouchy FBI agents stormed in, eyeballing Ethan and Becker like they had a thousand other things to do besides talk to them. They jerked out chairs from the other side of the conference table and sat, not looking at Ethan or Becker. Kept up a running banter on their side, something about the football games over the weekend.

Finally, they turned their way.

Ethan and Becker were officially read into the case. Mother was one spoke of an organized crime wheel that stretched across both the Canadian and Mexican borders, in big cities and small towns. She was a ghost, but she had left her touch across a dozen different major crime scenes. Ran prostitutes, who the FBI highly suspected were illegal immigrants. Ran drugs and money and counterfeited bills.

Girls connected to her had been found running weapons. But none had turned against her. They had no concrete leads. Not on her. Other angles of the investigation, yes. Mafia bosses in Chicago. Coyotes in New Mexico. Drug runners in Amarillo. But nothing on Mother.

"So we were told, by Headquarters, to listen to what you had to say," the first agent, a sour-faced man who looked like he was sucking on a lemon, said, glaring. "That you had something for us."

"We have an individual who will confirm that the three Jane Does are all connected to the human trafficking ring that brought her over the border. Our witness can also confirm all three girls' identities. And she's provided us with Mother's last known alias." Becker said, lacing his fingers together as he squared off against the agents across the table.

Silence. Pure, irrevocable silence.

19

Des Moines

They redirected all their energy, almost the entire team of agents and intelligence analysts at the secure site, to searching for Emily Jones, Mother's last known alias. A common name, with hundreds of possibilities across the Midwest, and then sent out agents to check up on each. Becker rode with the FBI agents in the field while Ethan worked operations and reviewed intelligence at the secure site. He cross-referenced what Gabriela had told them with the intel the FBI had gathered so far, trying to find new leads to pursue.

You should be out here.

Becker's text, late Monday afternoon, surprised him.

[You're doing great. You don't need me out there.]

But it's not fair.

He pulled together a few more possible leads for Becker and the FBI agents to run down and sent them over text. *[It is what it is. And you deserve this. How does investigations feel?]*

I love it. This is amazing. But you should be out here too.

[I'm good where I am.]

No luck on Monday. Becker stayed out with his team until just after eight at night. Ethan watched the clock, but Jack had already pushed back their call a few hours. He was still in the Situation Room—the final day before the invasion kicked off a furious frenzy of last-minute adjustments and intelligence gathering.

Finally, the FBI search teams called it quits for the day and promised to reconvene early Tuesday. Becker and Ethan shared a few words in the parking lot, but Becker kept looking down at his phone. Ethan knew what surreptitious texting looked like. He sent his young partner away and slid into his car.

When he'd gotten back the day before, his cupboards were empty, and his milk had gone sour again. He'd known as soon as he'd opened his refrigerator. The smell had slammed into him, and he'd shut the door quickly, coughing. An hour later, he took out the trash. He was left with some beer, ketchup, and an old packet of hot sauce.

He needed more food.

A quick text to the grocery store manager, and he turned his car toward the store by his apartment. He'd ditched the media following him that morning, leaving too early for them to show up outside his apartment. Blissfully, he was alone for the evening, not being stalked, not being followed. Like he was normal again.

The assistant manager was at the store, and he stood at the doors glaring at the parking lot when Ethan pulled in. He seemed shocked when it was just Ethan striding across the lot all alone, unmolested by photographers.

Ethan went through the store quickly, grabbing the essentials and making his way to the checkout. It was late and thankfully there was no one there to make snide comments or stare at him as he burned with frustration under their criticism. He dumped his basket on the checkout belt and pulled out his wallet as the checker scanned his groceries.

He could feel her eyes on him, though.

He looked up.

It was the same college girl from before, still chewing her gum. This time, though, she grinned at him.

He frowned. His gaze slid beyond her, to the magazines dotting the checkout lane and the newspapers in wire holders. On every cover, every front page, a picture of his and Jack's kiss at the airport burst from the sheets. On the gossip rags, shout lines clamored for attention beside the kiss. *Reconciliation! True Love Wins! Nothing Will Come Between Them!*

And on a newspaper, above the photo of their kiss, the bold headline declared: "Invasion's Good Luck Kiss."

He couldn't have kept in his smile if his life depended on it. He tried and ended up wrestling with his own lips, pursing and chewing on them as the college girl grinned. Ethan gave up and just smiled back.

"Twenty-four fifteen," she said, bagging his groceries. He slid his card and grabbed his bags. "Glad it's working out." She handed over the receipt and winked.

His cell buzzed on the way back to his car, and he fumbled the plastic bags around until he could pull it out.

Finally done for the day. Heading home. You up for a call?

[Always. Give me fifteen to get home from the store.]

Need to hear your voice. Talk to you soon, love.

Ethan sped a bit heading home, dumping his groceries as fast as he could, throwing lunch meat and vegetables into the fridge before heading for his computer. In moments, he was dialing Jack, and his lover answered with a haggard smile and messy hair, his tie undone as he leaned back on the bed. Weariness lined his gaze.

But he had Ethan's bear in his hands, held in his lap, and his smile grew brighter and less fatigued as they talked back and forth, well past midnight and into the early hours of the morning.

20

Jack's heart was ready to burst, beating out a terrible rhythm in his chest, a mixture of war drums and funeral lamentations, the wails of mourners and cries of rage and fury. Like an army of galloping horses or the clenching sobs of aching loss. He couldn't tell the difference anymore. It just ached, deeper than he'd ever ached before.

Jack breathed in and out, sitting at his desk in the Oval Office, listening to the silence. Silence was a rare thing as president. He had so few moments of true quiet. Moments where he tried to listen to himself think. Listen to his own thoughts and his own heart.

Were they doing the right thing?

Ethan believed in him and in what they were doing. He clung to that, to Ethan's certainty, and built his fragile house upon it.

He breathed in and out, again.

The phone rang. He dragged it close and picked up the handset, swallowing as he tried to force a lightness to his voice he just didn't feel. "Mr. President."

"*Mr. President.*" Sergey Puchkov's rolling voice echoed over the phone line. "*Are you ready to make history today? The first united American and Russian military engagement since World War II.*"

"I am ready to get this done."

Puchkov was quiet. "*We are doing the right thing. Righting a wrong that has been allowed to fester for too long. Too many have suffered for too long under the Caliphate. Iraq, and Syria… almost destroyed. The people there…*" Puchkov's sigh was ragged and tinged with sorrow.

He took a deep breath. "I know. In my heart, I know. If for nothing else than we're helping the people."

"*And stopping the spread of terror that is infecting the globe.*"

"Yes." His hand pressed against the desktop, fingers flattening. "There will be a cost, though."

"*There always is. I do not think I have to tell you that.*" Puchkov fell silent.

"No." Jack let out his breath, and the air crackled over the phone. "You don't."

"*We are in this together, Mr. President,*" Puchkov rumbled. "*We've joined in this, and our fates as presidents are now intertwined, for better or for worse.*"

"You'll be watching the invasion kickoff? Online and connected to our Situation Room?"

"*Of course. Our intelligence will be shared. Pick up the phone if you need me, Jack. For anything.*"

"You as well, Sergey. Good luck tonight. To you and your soldiers."

"*And to yours.*"

21

Des Moines

Phones ringing at the secured FBI site were a normal, common occurrence. Desk phones rang all day long, and the low murmur of conversations buzzing in the bullpen filled the air.

What *wasn't* usual was the way Agent Tyler paled, going ghost white before flushing a deep maroon and waving his hands over his head like he was on fire. He snapped his fingers, trying to draw attention, and covered the handset with his hand, hissing, "It's *her*! It's fucking her!"

Agents tripped over chairs and their own feet, trying to get to Tyler's desk first. He was manning the call-in line, taking tips from anyone who wanted to report what they might know about Emily Jones or the three girls' murders.

"Ms. Jones." Tyler cleared his throat, clenching his fist in front of his lips. "Why don't you come in and we can talk about things?"

He put her on speaker, but kept the microphone off. Only he could speak to her through the handset.

A throaty, cigarette-stained voice laughed, low and raspy. Her words, though, were lilting, almost musical. The hairs on the back of Ethan's neck rose. "*A nice gambit, Agent Tyler,*" Mother said. "*I would like to speak to Agent Reichenbach, please.*"

Every head turned his way. Eyes narrowed, glaring at him. Becker shuffled forward, elbowing an analyst out of the way to stand by Ethan. Even he side-eyed Ethan.

Tyler's face was purple. "Don't know anyone by that name."

She laughed.

"He's not authorized to speak on behalf of the investigation," Tyler growled. "You can deal with me."

"*I will speak to Agent Reichenbach or I will speak to no one. I want to deal, Agent Tyler. I want to work with you. But I will speak to him and him alone.*"

Silence. Tyler glared at him, fidgeting. One foot bounced, and his lips twisted as he mouthed a string of curses. Finally, he shoved the handset in Ethan's face.

Ethan cleared his throat. "Ms. Jones? What do you want with me?"

"*To talk. To meet. I will speak with you—and only you—tonight. Come to this bar—*" The other agents scrambled, diving for pens and paper to scrawl down what she said. "*I expect a whole team of federal agents will be there with you, Agent Reichenbach. But you'll be the only one who approaches me. And we'll talk.*"

"Why should I agree to this?" A thousand different scenarios were pouring through his mind, each more terrible than the last. Was this a setup? A hit? An attempted kidnapping? Some kind of publicity stunt, something that would hurt Jack?

"*It's the difference between cooperation and confrontation. I want to help you stop these murders. But you must give me something as well.*"

Part of him wanted to snap, to say that they didn't owe her shit. Not after three of her girls had been found dead. But she spoke before he could. "*I want justice for my girls.*"

He licked his lips. Glanced at Becker, who was shaking his head, his eyes wide. "How did you know I was on the investigation?" Everyone, from Smithson to Shepherd, would shit over this.

"*Our friend Gabriela,*" she said. There was a smile in her voice. "*See you tonight.*" The line cut out.

Becker lost his shit first, enough that Ethan steered him into a private conference room, away from the rest of the agents.

"You can't go!" Becker hollered. "Are you fucking *crazy*? With who you are? And the president?" Scoffing, Becker threw his hands in the air, pacing. "It's obviously a trap. A setup of some sort. Some kind of hit on you? That's a known mob bar!"

"Let's take it one step at a time—"

"One step at a time?" Becker wailed. "Until what? You step into a bullet?"

"I'll wear a vest."

"Doesn't do jack shit if they shoot you in the head." One finger wagged in Ethan's face. "And I'm *not* going to be the one to call the Goddamn president and tell him your big stupid ass is gone."

He chewed on the inside of his lip. Jack had more than enough to worry about with the invasion kicking off that night—still secretive knowledge, not released to the press, though the media was buzzing with anticipation. Jack had promised the operation would begin before the new year, and the days were numbered.

Should he even tell Jack about this?

Of course he had to. They didn't keep secrets. Didn't hide anything from one another. He wasn't about to start now. Not even with this.

"Why don't you go work with the teams planning site security? You can make sure the FBI actually does a halfway decent job of covering my ass."

Becker cursed, shaking his head as he glared. "Why?" he finally asked. "Why are you doing this?"

"'It's the difference between cooperation and confrontation,' she said. She wants to talk. She wants to help. She knows she's not getting out of that bar except in handcuffs—"

"Unless she's planning on executing you and you go down in a hail of bullets, along with her."

"Not her M.O." Ethan shook his head. "She's spent her entire life rescuing people. Even with everything she's accused of. Being part of this criminal underground. She's the Mother. Not the murderer."

"So say she's being manipulated by another mob boss to take you out, or the whole *investigation* out—"

Ethan held up his hand. "They're securing the premises now, unless they're entirely incompetent in their jobs." Ethan quirked a tiny smile. "And even though they're the FBI, they're not *that* bad. They'll be controlling the location. Nothing but agents in the bar. It's not like walking into a viper's den."

"I still don't like it."

"Indulging her for a moment will cost very little. And maybe gain everything. I'm meeting her."

Becker sighed. "I'll be on the other end of the radio."

Jack wasn't thrilled with the news, but he didn't try to stop Ethan either. He asked question after question about the security plans, trying to understand exactly how Ethan would be protected. Wanted to know more about Mother and why she was worth him going to speak to her. They hadn't spoken much about Ethan's case over Christmas, and now he gave Jack a rundown of how he'd sneaked off and chatted with Smithson and how they had the key to possibly breaking open a huge criminal underground in the Midwest.

"*Just be careful, Ethan,*" Jack breathed. "*I trust your judgment. But I don't want you to get hurt.*"

"I will be careful. And I'll still be here for you. During the—" He shrugged. "You know."

A heavy exhale was all he heard.

Hours later, he waited in the back of the tactical undercover minivan, wearing jeans and his bulletproof vest under a sweatshirt Becker had picked up for him that afternoon, something bulky from Iowa State University. He had a mic taped below his collarbone and the battery pack secured to the inside of his waistband.

Becker had flushed when he'd helped Ethan tape the mic to his chest and found the fading remnants of a kiss bruise Jack had left during their last morning together.

A few agents were sitting around the empty bar, wearing plainclothes and sipping sodas. The regular bartender was sitting in a jail cell, cooling his heels and thinking about a bench warrant issued last year. An FBI agent had taken his place. The bar was theirs, as was the parking lot, filled with cars stuffed full of agents trying to surreptitiously stare at tablets and cell phones in the dark.

Close to ten PM, a ratty sedan pulled in, and a middle-aged woman headed for the door. Her hair was dark and cut in a bob. She had a long, worn coat on and jeans tucked into boots that crunched through the snow, the sound echoing through the silent parking lot.

Everyone waited until she was inside the bar. Becker clapped him on the shoulder, holding Ethan's gaze. "Good luck." He tapped his ear. "I'm online."

Ethan smiled at his partner. "See you soon."

He hopped out of the minivan and into the frigid December night. They'd parked farther from the door than Mother had, and he skidded a bit on snow that had frozen over, a slick sheen of ice underfoot. He blew on his hands before he opened the door to the bar and pulled back his hoodie as he ducked inside.

Scattered around the room, the undercover agents obsessively didn't look his way.

The one woman at the bar, however, did.

Mother smiled wide. She tapped the bar top, beckoning him over, and then shrugged out of her coat. "Right on time."

He joined her. The FBI agent behind the bar stared at them both as he wiped down glassware that was already clean and dry.

"Mother?"

"Emily Jones." She held her hand out, and he shook it. "But you already know that."

"From our friend Gabriela."

She smiled and pulled a pack of cigarettes from her back pocket. She offered one to Ethan and lit her own when he declined. "She's a sweet one. Got mixed up bad with that dumbass with the mullet, but there's no stopping young hearts when they think they've found love."

179

"You taught her how to counterfeit, right? She brought the know-how to his little gang?"

"She's a smart cookie. I had her help out once or twice. She learned how to put two and two together, and when she left, she took a few things from me to set up her own operation." A long drag on the cigarette. "Kids, you know." She winked.

Despite himself, Ethan chuckled.

The bartender glared.

"But she was cutting into someone else's turf and they didn't like that. Someone new. Someone who wanted to make a statement." Spinning toward the bar top, Mother rested her elbows on the polished wood. "She caught the attention of these people. It's good she's in jail." Mother nodded slowly. "She'll be safer there. And—" she leaned into Ethan's shoulder. "She's going to cooperate fully with your investigation now."

"Oh yeah?"

"Yep. I spoke to her about it."

Ethan's eyebrows climbed high on his forehead. "Spoke to her?"

"Honey, please." Mother sucked another deep inhale of her cigarette. "How do you think I knew you were all looking for me? And you in particular."

"What's this about?" He leveled a flat stare her way. "Why are we here?"

She blew her smoke in his face. He didn't move.

"It's funny. You can't spit these days without hitting some mention of you somewhere. You're famous, Reichenbach."

He blinked.

"For your choices. What you *chose* to do. What was right, what was wrong, and how you navigated in between." Another long drag, and ash fell from the end of her crackling cigarette. "You come off as a hard piece of shit, and I haven't seen you smile once. Until this past weekend." She grinned.

"We're not here to talk about me. If you just want to stare, you should have gone to the zoo."

"You get it," she said. One hand landed on his arm, warm through his sweatshirt. "You get hard choices. You understand how those are made."

The air seemed to vibrate a little differently, the lights dimmer around the edges as he tried to swallow past his clenching throat.

"You helped Gabi come to the right decision, even though it cut out her heart to give you my name. And you cared for her through it. I know it doesn't mean much, the admiration of a prostitute and a criminal, but you've got a fan in her, Reichenbach. You're a real Prince Charming to that little lady."

His mind stuck on her words. His eyes narrowed. "The right decision?"

"Mm." She waved to the bartender, sucking down the last of her cigarette. "Two beers please. Something dark."

The bartender stared. He didn't move.

Sighing, she stared at Ethan. "How do you think this is going to end tonight, Reichenbach? Another shoot-out like the one in the Oval Office? A raging car chase through the slums? Holding a bullet wound tight as you imagine your lover calling your name?"

Around the bar, wooden chairs squeaked across the floor, agents readying to stand, reaching for their hips.

Mother grinned, almost sadly, one corner of her mouth quirking up as she snuffed out her cigarette in a glass dish. "This isn't that kind of story," she said. "No raging gun battles. No shoot-out at the O.K. Corral. This one is just about hard choices and doing things for the ones we love."

Silence. No one moved in the bar.

"So I'm going to turn myself in," Mother said softly. "And I'm going to turn in all my girls, too. Get them off the streets."

"Who is killing them? Who is hunting them?"

"Rival mob boss. Eastern European. He moved into Chicago and he's been moving his way out from the city. Gabriela started counterfeiting and ran into turf he'd claimed as his own. He took offense and tracked down her friends. Now he's coming after me. It's all tangled up out here, you see." She looked down, squinting. "He's coming after girls who are mine."

"You ran your girls as prostitutes?"

"Don't judge." Mother pulled out another cigarette, lighting it as she spoke. "Until you've been where they've been and have no other choices than what they had, don't judge."

"I'm the last one to judge on bad choices made with no options."

She chuckled, smoke falling from her chapped lips. "I'll give you everything about these guys. Who they are. Where they are. What they're up to. Who they're working with."

Somewhere across the bar, a glass dropped, shattering on the ground. One of the undercover agents at the table cursed, and another kicked him.

Mother smiled. "One thing. You know my girls are running fake identities." Ethan nodded.

"I'm going to tell you they're all underage."

His breath punched from his lungs as his jaw dropped. "You're going to admit to running an *underage* prostitution ring? You realize you'll be in jail for the rest of your life?"

She shrugged, taking another drag. "Sure I will." Exhale. "But they'll be taken into protective custody instead of jail. Treated, instead of incarcerated. Given new lives, instead of punished for their former ones. And they won't be in danger of being killed anymore."

Ethan sagged. "They're not underage, are they?"

"You guys really going to go through the trouble of trying to prove they're not? Or you just gonna take care of them? Especially when they cooperate so nicely with you all?"

He turned away from her and back toward the bar. Gripped the wooden edge until his fingers ached. "Hey," he grunted to the agent working the bar. "Bring us those beers."

The undercover agent glowered at him but stomped off when Ethan glared right back. He slid two bottles down the bar top and crossed his arms, no longer pretending not to watch.

Ethan unscrewed both tops and passed one to Mother. She smiled her thanks, raising her beer in a toast.

"You're unconventional. I like that," she said after she'd drunk. "I bet that's why you and he fit so well together."

"Who?"

"President Spiers. Your boyfriend." She winked as Ethan choked on his next swallow. "He's unconventional, too. That's why I voted for him."

He finally chuckled, sliding his beer bottle back and forth across the wood grain. "You're willing to go down for this? They're going to throw the book at you. It won't be good."

"No, it won't be." Another drag, and she tapped the ashes off into the dish. "I've done enough, though, to earn the time. I'll plead guilty. And this is what you do when you love the hard way. Make those kinds of choices that no one else can make." Smoke wafted from her lips as she spoke. "You understand."

"I do."

She held out her beer bottle for another clink of the longnecks. "What do you say we finish these beers and then you can have those men over in that booth arrest me?" She grinned around her cigarette. They both drank, leaning against the bar top side by side.

"You're a good man, Reichenbach," she finally said, draining the last of her beer. "It's why he loves you."

He didn't answer her. Instead, he set their bottles on the bar and fished out a twenty, leaving it for the bar owner when he returned. "Are you ready?"

"Yeah, I suppose so. This is the way it's gonna go. This is the way they're all saved." Sighing, she straightened and looked him dead in the eyes. "Thank you for what you did with Gabi." She turned to the FBI agents rising from the corner booth. "Howdy, boys. Ready?"

He stepped back while they read her rights and placed the cuffs on her wrists. She didn't resist, and when they walked her toward the door, she sent one last smile Ethan's way. "Keep fighting the good fight. Follow your own path."

He watched through the windows as she was loaded into the van and the last of her cigarette fell to ash and whispering smoke on the edge of the glass dish.

22

White House

The invasion kicked off at precisely eleven PM Washington DC time, six AM in Iraq.

US paratroopers jumped into Iraq from Turkey and Jordan and Russian troopers from Georgia and Azerbaijan in the predawn darkness. Thousands of troopers filled the sky and swarmed on the ground, meeting up before moving across the desert and making the first strike of the invasion. Overhead, air strikes and artillery paved the way for ground forces moving in.

In the Situation Room, adrenaline made the air heavy, stinking with tension and sweat. Jack watched everything on the monitors from the head of the table. His generals and their aides buzzed, answering phones and fielding messages and dispatches from the invasion, working up the chain. A constant hum and a frisson thrummed the air. Jack fiddled with the watch Ethan had given him, running his fingers over the face and around the band.

Just after midnight, General Bradford took a call on a cell phone passed by one of his attachés. He grunted into the phone and then sighed, long and low. His head fell forward. Jack's gaze flicked to him and held.

Bradford passed the phone back to his aide. He turned to Jack. "Mr. President, we have our first confirmed K-I-A."

Jack's blood froze. Everything within him stopped, his whole body turning to ice in an instant as the world slammed to a screeching halt.

He knew this would happen. Knew they would lose soldiers, lose good people in this fight. He'd known from the second he had committed to this course that this exact moment would happen. He could push the dread off for days, wrap himself up in the arguments that they were doing this all for the right reasons. They had the moral high ground. They had the whole world backing them up, a multinational coalition that spanned the globe and the blessings of the UN. This was the right and just thing to do, for so many.

But he couldn't quite silence the young man inside of him who had lost his wife in the war all those years ago. Or the older man who had buried Ethan in Arlington, supposedly due to the Caliphate's attack in Ethiopia.

Another family was going to feel like that now. Another family was going to have their heart ripped out, and have to accept a folded flag.

Dread had consumed him since Ethan had left and the reality of what they were about to do sank down upon him again. Without Ethan's bulwark, that heavy weight was hovering, threatening to crash down upon him.

"Who?" Jack breathed.

"Private Kevin Rodriguez. 82nd Airborne out of Fort Bragg. Infantry. Nineteen years old. His family lives in Los Angeles."

Jack closed his eyes. He'd be writing letters soon, letters to the families of fallen soldiers. The first one would go to California.

"It's being released to the media in a few hours."

"Thank you, General. Lawrence—" He turned to his chief of staff. "Have Pete put a statement together for the media." The soldier's name would be held back until the family was notified, but they still needed to say something. He needed to say something, for his own sanity and for his soul.

Swallowing, he pushed himself to his feet. Pressed his hands to the tabletop. "I'm going to take a walk. I'll be back in a few minutes."

He escaped the Situation Room, silent after the general's announcement. The heavy door slammed shut behind him and he walked away, heading down the hall to the West Wing's ground-floor lobby. Mostly used by journalists and the press pool, the lobby was empty after midnight, still in the dead hours. He was alone, save for his Secret Service shadows hanging back out of sight.

He sank into one of the stuffed blue chairs beneath a picture of President Kennedy and pinched the bridge of his nose. Across from him, a bronze sculpture of Marines raising the flag on Iwo Jima rested atop a hand-carved wooden dresser from Lincoln's presidency. History, so much history, and men who had come before him.

Who had made excruciating decisions and had to live with them. How? How had they gotten through?

His hands fumbled in his pockets, searching for his cell phone. The phone shook as he pulled it out, and he realized it wasn't the phone. It was him. He was trembling. He dialed, punching in Ethan's number as he leaned forward and braced his elbows on his knees.

"Jack?" Ethan picked up on the first ring. *"Everything all right?"*

"Hey, love." Jack's throat seized. He licked his lips, blinking fast as his eyes blurred.

"Hey. How's it going? I've got the news on. Not much is being reported right now, aside from that it's started."

He nodded, as if Ethan could see him. Finally cleared his throat. "So far, the invasion is going well. According to plan." He sniffed, one hand rubbing down his face, covering his mouth. "We just had our first K-I-A," he whispered.

Silence. *"Jack. I'm sorry. God, I'm sorry. I know how this hits you."*

Nodding, again. He couldn't speak, not just yet. And he was losing the battle against his blurring eyes, against the tears that threatened to fall. One cascaded down his cheek. He wiped it away. "I've got to write a letter to his family. I remember getting mine. I hated it so *much*. So trite. So... cold." He took a slow breath. "There's going to be more."

"What can I do? How can I help?"

"Just— Just need to hear your voice." He cleared his throat. Wiped at his eyes and sniffed again. "Tell me about your day. Thank you for the text telling me you're alive and everything went well."

"She turned herself in. Wanted to give herself up in exchange for us protecting her girls."

"She was a madam, right?"

"Of a sort. But that's the FBI's case. Tomorrow, I'm back on counterfeiting. That's not our mystery to solve."

"But you did great work. Helped put things together. Connected people, and hopefully more people will be saved out there."

Ethan was quiet. *"Like what you're doing over there? Connecting the world and putting a stop to those evils? Saving lives?"*

Dammit. Jack closed his eyes as his lips quivered.

"Hard choices require hard love. The kind of love that sometimes hurts it runs so deep. You have that kind of love for the world, Jack. And for everybody." Ethan's voice had dropped, rougher and deeper. *"You are a good man."*

His feet bounced, and another tear slipped down his cheek, but he left it. "Thank you," he whispered. "If I'm half as good a man as you believe I am, I'll take that."

"You're more, love."

"I'm a better man with you. With your love."

"Likewise."

Down the hall, in the direction of the Situation Room, a shadow moved. Jack squinted, watching it veer toward him. The shape of a man appeared, one of his aides poking his head into the lobby. "Mr. President, phone call for you in the Situation Room. President Puchkov."

"Gotta go, love. Duty calls." He stood and nodded to his aide, wiping at his eyes and rubbing his nose as he straightened his tie. Tried to put himself back together and become the president once again.

"Call me anytime. I'm here for you. Always."

"Thanks." He sniffed for the last time, exhaling slowly. "I love you."

"Love you too."

23

Des Moines

When he got in Wednesday morning, Ethan found a Post-It stuck to his computer monitor. *See me immediately.* Sighing, Ethan grabbed the note and headed to Shepherd's office.

"You called?" He held the note up, stuck to one finger.

"Shut the door."

Shepherd was all business, sitting at his desk and waiting for Ethan to take a seat before he spoke. "I'm not going to pretend I don't know what you've been up to these past few days. I knew Monday morning when the head of the FBI office called me, screaming about how I needed to bench you and strip you of your badge and gun."

Ethan stayed quiet.

"I wanted to see how this would play out. What you guys would do. You had a real shot at ending this thing." Shepherd tapped his desktop. "And you did. Well done."

Stunned, Ethan blinked at his supervisor. "Sir?"

"You refused to take the easy way out, Reichenbach. You kept doing your job. Kept showing up. Kept being an agent." Shepherd shrugged. "I was wrong about you."

Ethan's jaw dropped.

Shepherd cleared his throat. "That FBI head called me back. Said he's got an opening on his JTTF team and wants to offer it to this office." He squinted. "You want to restart your career? You probably can't run an investigation in your own name, but you can do everything else. Run intel and counterintel. Work with the others. Chase terrorists. Go after the big fish again." One hand waved over his desk and out his windows to the bullpen of agents. "Not be stuck here working financial crimes."

Stunned, Ethan watched Shepherd carefully, waiting to see if this was all some big joke. If Shepherd was that cruel. Shepherd just blinked at him.

A spot on the regional Joint Terrorism Task Force. That wasn't just a career restart, it was a career surge. He'd be right in the thick of everything again. Agents on the JTTF shot up the ranks, and they were vanguards for the nation and the world. The front line of law enforcement against terrorists—any terrorists—who wanted to strike.

Long hours. Long days. Perhaps missed weekends. The job would cut into his time with Jack, of that he had no doubt. Would take away from his relationship with Jack.

Was that what he wanted? Where did he want to put his effort? His devotion? Was rebuilding his career really—truly—what he wanted? At the cost of losing time—irreplaceable time—with Jack?

Financial crimes wasn't sexy, but it was stable. He had his daily hours. His routine. And every Friday, he was on the way to Jack. That, more than anything else, *mattered* to him.

He licked his lips and cleared his throat before he spoke. "I think," he said slowly, "there's a better agent suited to that position."

Shepherd's eyebrows rose. "You wanna give this to Becker?"

"He's a good kid. This is where he wants to grow. And it's a great opportunity. Becker should get the job, sir."

"I don't have another babysitter for you in the office. You'll be working alone after this."

Ethan smiled. The rest of his colleagues were older than he was, agents on the way to retirement. No one who needed mentorship, or guidance, or a hand to show them the ropes. He heard what Shepherd said, between his caustic words. "That's all right. I'm good on my own."

"All right." Shepherd tapped his desk again. "I'll let him know. Oh, and—" He stood, sighing like he was tired and no amount of sleep would help with that. "I'm giving you the rest of the week off. You're out of vacation, but take this as comp time. You did good on this case. You deserve a few days. I don't want to see you until Monday."

Shepherd couldn't be serious. There had to be a catch. "Sir, do you expect me to remain on recall for the—"

"Get the hell out of here, Reichenbach! I expect you to be on the way to the airport soon!"

"Yes, sir." He hesitated at the door. "Thank you, Shepherd."

Shepherd waved him away.

Ethan made record time logging out of his workstation and heading out, zooming back to his apartment. He threw some clothes into his duffel, grabbed his cell phone charger, and barreled out the door.

On the way to the airport, his phone rang. It was Becker.

"What's up?"

"Hey, where are you? I've been looking for you."

"Heading out of town. Shepherd gave me some comp days. I'm on the way to the airport."

"Shit." Becker grunted. *"Well, I guess I'll tell you over the phone, then. He just promoted me."* Becker sounded amazed, like he couldn't believe what he was saying. *"He reassigned me to the JTTF. Can you believe that?"*

"Congratulations, man. You deserve it. I'm happy for you."

"Fucking amazing."

He could hear the smile in Becker's voice.

"I was going to ask if you wanted to come out for drinks with Ellie and me, but..." Becker trailed off.

"Sorry. On the way to DC."

"Sure. Yeah. I, uh. I start on Monday. So... I won't see you at the office anymore."

Ethan sighed. He'd most likely never see Becker again. Not when Becker made new friends and dove into his job and started dating Ellie for real. "Maybe some other time, Blake."

"Yeah. I'll... I'll see you around, Reichenbach. Stay out of trouble."

He laughed. "You know me."

Becker snorted, and the line cut out.

He paid for his ticket to DC at the counter and made his way through security before any media showed up. He waited at the coffee shop, tapping his foot as he sipped his latte and nodded to his federal shadow, who arrived thirty minutes later, wide-eyed and surprised. A fresh cup of coffee was waiting for his shadow at the counter.

Finally, just before boarding began, he pulled out his phone and texted Jack. *[Can you talk?]*

Give me a minute.

His phone rang.

"Hey, love."

"*Hey.*" Jack sounded ragged, like he hadn't slept at all. "*What's up?*"

"I'm on my way. I'm coming to DC. Shepherd gave me some time off, so I'm coming out there."

"*What...*"

The call for boarding started, and Ethan hefted his duffel. "I don't want you to have to write those letters to the families alone, Jack. I'm coming out there for you. I want to be with you for this." He passed his ticket to the boarding agent and headed down the ramp onto the plane. He'd bought a coach ticket, not first class, and he made his way to the back. "Is that all right?"

"*Ethan...*" Jack sounded breathless, shocked and pilloried, but wonder ran through his tone. "*Ethan—*" His voice choked off, and he coughed, clearing his throat. "*When do you get in?*"

"Three thirty. I texted Scott. He's sending someone." Ethan shoved his duffel overhead and sat in his seat, buckling himself in as the first passengers filed onboard.

"*Ethan...God, I'm so glad you're coming. I need you right now.*"

"I love you, Jack. And I'm with you all the way."

Interlude: First Noel

About the Author

Tal Bauer is an award-winning and best-selling author of LGBT romantic thrillers, bringing together a career in law enforcement and international humanitarian aid to create dynamic characters, intriguing plots, and exotic locations. He is happily married and lives with his husband and their Basset Hound in Texas. Tal is a member of the Romance Writers of America and the Mystery Writers of America.

Other Books By Tal Bauer

Please visit your favorite ebook retailer to discover my other books.

The Executive Office Series
Enemies of the State
Interlude
Enemy of My Enemy
Enemy Within

Hush

Connect With Tal Bauer

Visit my website: www.talbauerwrites.com
Email me: tal@talbauerwrites.com
Friend me on Facebook:
https://www.facebook.com/talbauerauthor
Follow me on Twitter: @TalBauerWrites

Made in the USA
Las Vegas, NV
25 November 2024

12599603R00115